Viennese Short Stories

Canetti was no casual bystander or disinterested witness to the defeat of Austrian social democracy. In January 1934, she had already been threatened with deportation because of her work with the paper: although a native of Vienna, she held a Yugoslav passport following the collapse of the Habsburg Monarchy at the end of the First World War. On the night of 12 February, she sheltered two prominent Social Democratic leaders, Ernst Fischer and Ruth von Mayenburg, who would soon become leaders of the anti-Nazi resistance. Both describe the night in their memoirs.[6] They left the next morning because Canetti was so well known to the authorities.

These experiences feed into "Three Heroes and a Woman," in which she commemorates the February events with typically defiant optimism. Another deceptively simple tale, this time featuring a cool-headed cleaning woman outwitting three Viennese police officers, it was published in July 1934 next to contributions by Brecht, Stefan Heym, and Max Brod in Herzfelde's Prague-based *Neue Deutsche Blätter*, her only known connection with the exiled German-speaking anti-Nazis. Such exalted literary company was nothing new. The *Arbeiter-Zeitung* had also published original literary writing by writers such as Kästner, Joseph Roth, and Ernst Toller.

Even though Dollfuß had triumphed, he still faced opposition from the Nazis, who from the summer of 1933 had been attempting to destabilize his regime by acts of terrorist sabotage. In "New Boy," Canetti's last *Arbeiter-Zeitung* story in November 1933, the naively well-intentioned seller of "red" newspapers covers up for his "brown" colleague after the police have found explosives in his flat. Yet, as Austria stared political cataclysm in the face, Canetti evoked working-class solidarity which transcended allegiance to the "brown" (that is, Nazi) or "red" (social-democrat) camps. They have more in common than what artificially divides them.

Canetti's nom de plume, Veza Magd, became her political battle cry because she saw into the minds of Vienna's enormous army of domestic servants. As a writer herself, she also regarded herself as a servant, a domestic serving maid or *Magd*. In "The Poet," she sets out what she expects from anyone who deserves to be called one. The poet in question is male, like the writer in "Clairvoyants," and poor. As a child, he knows no better than to eat dirt with his bread when it falls to the ground. He is brought up by his mother, who spends the summer working in the fields and the winter at home on her knitting machine. His poverty makes him an outsider: he is shunned by the landowner's children, who are forbidden to speak to him, and he stands out from his classmates at school, who think themselves better than him. He is the only one in the group who does not know what he wants to be when he grows up, but he does well at school and, as a young man, he shows a talent for teaching and a fanatical sense of justice. When his superiors ask him to write down his method, they discover that he has the stuff of a poet in him and send him away to write his life story. Now he returns to his home town to write the story of his life.

Elias Canetti wrote of Veza's faith in poets. In "The Poet," writing is dependent on experience and is linked to justice, teaching, and overcoming poverty. In "Clairvoyants," the writer who narrates the story is the only person who sees through the charlatan who pretends he can read the minds of his audience. As the charlatan clairvoyant is an analogy for Hitler, the narrator shows that a writer using his reason can dispel the hold which a demagogue exercises over his audience.

The contrast with the other poet who is featured in this book is stark. Knut Tell, the subject of "Lost Property," is also a character in the first chapter of *Yellow Street* and in Canetti's second play, *The Tiger*, where he finally is portrayed much more positively than in either story. He is taken to be Canetti's satirical, love-hate portrait of her husband-to-be. In "Lost Property," Tell is persuaded by his patient, long-suffering girlfriend to take a job at the city lost-property office with the promise that he is bound to find new literary material. On the evening of his first day, he falls in love with a character he has been inspired to create after meeting a young working-class woman who has been spurned in love by a hospital doctor. Unlike the true poet, Tell puts his story first and does not care about the rejected Fräulein Adenberger. He acts as if he wants to return her handbag but is really fascinated by the piece of writing, the draft of her letter to Doctor Spanek contained in the bag. The ungrammatical German in which she writes her appeal makes her case all the more intriguing. For Tell, her story and the language she uses to express it are just literary fodder. His appropriation of her story is unethical and contrasts directly with Gustl's use of his own experience in "The Poet."

Veza Canetti's style evolved quickly and grew in subtlety. After her avenues of publication were blocked, she changed her approach in order to get into print again. She shows her command of the traditional short-story form in all three stories published in 1937. "Hush Money" hinges on a chambermaid at a high-class sanatorium misunderstanding why she is given a 100-schilling note wrapped up in a pair of panties belonging to a baroness. Canetti extracts all she can from the sexual farce before turning the text into a morality tale. The baroness's lover, moreover, is a Hitler look-alike, described as "an imposing gentleman with a tiny black moustache, who, for reasons which were known only to himself, always wore riding breeches." His origins and need for treatment are unknown, making him: "the object of more speculation among the patients in the *Lilienhain* Sanatorium than even the consultant. They said he was not seriously ill at all but had reasons for hiding himself away. Politics, whispered the psychiatric cases; on account of someone's husband, averred the moderately ill. Because of his splendid appearance, they called him the *Magnate*." (Canetti's italics)

This description is tucked away in the middle of what the censor would have assumed is a harmless story about rich women falling in love with their doctor. The chambermaid is the only character to emerge with her integrity intact.

The stories collected in this volume were all published in the German-speaking press between June 1932 and May 1937. Apart from two others which became chapters in *Yellow Street* ("The Canal" and "A Child Rolls Gold"), they represent the sum of Veza Canetti's published output during her lifetime. The last story, "Money - Money - Money," has something of the folk or fairy tale in the way it tells of the conflict between a miserly, meat-devouring ogre who bullies his family and burns his money so that they cannot inherit it and the unassuming maid who hastens his death by feeding him ever greater quantities of the unhealthy fare he demands. The basic elements are timeless. Yet, the story is embedded just as closely in historical reality as Canetti's others, if not more so. The action spans the First World War and the economic hardship, food shortages, and inflation the war brought in its train. As it incorporates Canetti's own self-assertion against domestic oppression, it is also her most personal story. In other ways, it is the most political of all the stories published here: her subject is patriarchal power and its subjugation of the weak in its pursuit of its own advantage. The revenge of the maid is the revenge of the oppressed everywhere. On 1 May 1937, readers of the censored *Die Stunde* would not have needed any help to decode its contemporary message. Its author must have felt quietly victorious. Getting the story into print was a triumph similar to the maid's, but it was to be Veza Canetti's last. Until her death in a Hampstead hospital precisely twenty-six years later, she found it impossible to publish another story, whether in British exile or in democratically restored Austria after 1945.

Julian Preece
University of Kent

Notes

1. Dorothee Wierling, *Mädchen für alles. Arbeitsalltag und Lebensgeschichte städtischer Dienstmädchen um die Jahrhundertwende* (Berlin/Bonn: Dietz, 1987) has sub-chapters on all these topics. See also Karin Walser, *Dienstmädchen, Frauenarbeit und Weiblichkeitsbilder um 1900* (Frankfurt aM: Neue Kritik, 1986), especially pp. 59-80.

2. Unpublished chapter of *The Torch in the Ear* (1980), "Trauer und Verlockung" ("Mourning and Enticement"), deposited with Elias Canetti's papers in the Zurich Zentralbibliothek, box no. 226.

3. The Universum-Film AG (Ufa) was founded in December 1917 to produce wartime propaganda. After the war and until the Nazi takeover in 1933, the company produced such cinematic masterpieces as *Metropolis* (dir. Fritz Lang) and *The Blue Angel* (dir. Josef von Sternberg) and competed with Hollywood for market share in Europe. The studio was taken over in 1927 by the media baron, Alfred Hugenberg, an enthusiastic supporter of Adolf Hitler, and by 1932, when Albers was already in his pomp, was no longer making films of distinction.

The Victor[1]

One is not always reminded of Werther's Lotte when hungry children stand around their sister waiting for bread.[2] When Anna distributed bread, it seemed different. Her brothers and sisters may have stood around her, but they were more absorbed by the bread itself than by the favor of receiving it from her. Nor did she joke as she cut the bread, as she was full of worries. Seven souls had to satisfy their hunger and bread was their only staple.

The father, Anna's father, looked as if the weight of all the parcels, boxes, errands, and curses still bore down on him after he had finished work. Even in his own eyes, he was the lowliest servant of the firm Hessel & Co., where boss, directors, bookkeepers, typing girls, and clerks all used to bully him if they were in a bad temper. His constant state of harassment only made their tempers worse. Thus burdened by the troubles of those above him, he came home every evening and saw in his numerous children only demanding stomachs who ate into his meager wage.

The mother could not get work as a servant because seven souls gave her enough work to do. Her blue-striped housecoat hung loosely over her gaunt figure, the lines about her mouth were taut, and only her eyes belied her life of misery. They were so bright and constant that her children would always look for her gaze which fed them with hope for better times. Mrs. Seidler had retained this joyfulness because she did not suffer the harassment her husband did, so endlessly, pointlessly, hopelessly. On the contrary, she watched how her children flourished under her care and she often wondered how little healthy children could naturally make do with and how people grew bigger from potatoes, dumplings, bread, and fat and had eyes which were alert, bones which were strong, and breath which was quick.

One hundred schillings a month, exactly the same amount as her father, was what Anna earned, and, just like her father, she handed it over. Mrs. Seidler admired the progress which young people had made, a nineteen-year-old who earned so much.

Anna worked in a cloth factory, where everything from flax

to yarn, from cotton to thread was manufactured. In the first year, Anna sat on the floor and checked the cloth. She separated pure linen from the mixed fabrics, and that was where her trouble began. Torn or knotted threads had to be pulled out with a needle and carefully replaced. The white wool dust which filled the air dried out her eyes and lungs.

After a year she was given easier work. Now all she had to do was mark where the cloth was damaged with a blue pen. True, she had to stand at the same spot for eight hours, but it was easier. Anna found it too easy. She peeped at the next-door room where the rattle of the machines was deafening and would have liked to have been in charge of one. That was important, responsible, and exciting, and it brought in twenty schillings extra, and who knew what a difference twenty schillings could make?

After another year, her dream came true. She moved to the department with machines. She still wore the same dress made from dark material and looked earnestly at the women who painted cheerfulness onto their faces in bright makeup. She did not look at them critically but with that reserve which poverty and a sense of duty impose. She took charge of the machine and wore a rubber hat to stop the quickly rotating blades from catching in her hair, which was long and done up in a bun.

In the evening she read her old schoolbooks. She wanted to educate herself so that there would be enough of the fresh bread that she distributed so carefully each day. Work by day, work in the evenings, and work on Sundays to relieve her mother. As no color ever came into the monotony of her life her countenance became sorrowful like her father's.

Upstairs on the floor with the fine offices, the workforce was being reduced. The foreman, Mr. Atila, went through the rooms to get help from below, looked at the girls, and his gaze fell on Anna, who looked back at him with her blue, lifeless eyes, like a faithful dog. He waved her over into the next-door room because you could not hear yourself speak in the machine department, and from this moment Anna worked upstairs. She lined up the bales in a row, attached labels to them, and soon she had the numbering for all the various types of cloth in her head. Whenever Mr. Boar telephoned to find out the code for something like the blue-striped demi-canvas, Anna called the answer across to the boss on the telephone, and Mr. Boar was served promptly. There were invoices to be got in, orders to be copied, bills to be checked, and in the evening the floor had to be swept. One thing, though, provided Anna with unutterable happiness. Every morning she came in an hour earlier than the others, sat down at the typewriter, and began to type. The letters jumped, formed a line, caused confusion, and were soon under her control. And one day the miracle happened. When the boss was so busy upstairs and down-stairs that he did not know whether he was coming or going, Anna sat herself down, the daughter of the shop assistant Seidler, three years of secondary school and now nothing, and she wrote the letters.

From that point on, she did simply everything. She was so useful that her name was known in several rooms like that of a factotum. On her way home, her blue eyes looked out warmly onto the world. But no man in the tram ever looked twice at her. For she had that impure complexion, those permanently reddened eyes, which had become chronic, she had a broad nose, and still wore that dark-colored dress.

The boss of the Salzman factory, Siegfried Salzman, walked around with a head full of worries. The value of sterling was unfavorable and the company had debts. All foreign currencies were in fact unstable, and before Siegfried Salzman let go of his fine linen in return for scraps of paper of dubious value, he preferred to wait a little longer and not to sell at all. He was literally sitting on his wares. Of course, this meant work came to a standstill and the workforce was cut again.[3] They started downstairs in the workers' section before it was the turn of the upstairs floor. On the upstairs floor Siegfried Salzman himself wanted to separate the capable from the incapable. He went through the rooms and took a look at the girls. There was Miss Loach, a redhead, who had great influence on her workmates, she had to be kept on, she would kick up a fuss otherwise. There was Miss Fungus, who despite her hunchback was very useful, she reported to the boss all sorts of things the employees had said. Then there was Käthe Schmidt, he recognized her from behind, as he had seduced her already. And Salzman wetted his lips and his fat face grew larger when he saw Daisy Sparrow, seventeen years old and built very daintily. He thought how sweet she had been that time he had given her strong wine to drink. He went

further, and one after another came girls who had surrendered to
him the blossom of their youth, which the daughters of the
welloff sell for a high price, for an evening meal, and – even
more important – for the great advantage which came from the
boss's goodwill. None of these girls, decided Siegfried Salzman,
shall lose her job. And then he saw a figure which he did not
know from behind. His eyes rested on the girl's full legs.
Although clothed in cheap ribbed stockings, something roundly
youthful attracted him to the calves, and he stepped forward
briskly. He saw a spotty complexion, reddened eyes, a broad
nose, and a hunched figure.

One hour later the foremen were called in to see him.

"Anna Seidler?" said Mr. Atila, "but she's the best worker
I've got!"

"She's grumpy," said the cloth manufacturer.

How should she not be grumpy with the poverty at home,
thought the foreman, but he did not say anything as he had a
family to feed himself. And that was that. When Anna went into
the boss's office, she could not help herself. All her misery rose
to the surface, made her eyes even redder, and ran through her
nose. These tears irritated the boss. And because he had a good
heart, he wrote her a glowing reference.

The Great Tormentor is concerned that his material should
not go to wrack and ruin, and so fate bequeathed Anna a new
position. The practiced eye of Chief Clerk Raven picked her out
from among thirty applicants, for he did not like any distractions
in his business. He read through her reference with satisfaction,
and suddenly something occurred to him.

"It does not say here that you have any secretarial experience,
Miss."

Anna asserted shyly that she did, and we know that she was
not lying.

"Then kindly bring a new reference and you will be hired."

Overjoyed, Anna promised to do so, did not sleep, wrote a
letter to the boss during the night, and took it in personally in the
morning. Her cold hands were damp from excitement as she
stood in front of the foreman. He found her request so trifling
that he went to the boss straightaway, glad that his conscience no
longer needed to weigh down on him because he had spoken up
for the hard-working woman.

Siegfried Salzman sat behind his grand writing desk chewing sticks of gum. Next to him lay a magnificent greyhound. He kept a special chef in the factory for this greyhound as the beast was a fussy eater.

"Three first prizes," Salzman was just saying when Mr. Atila entered. After making a bow he presented his request with that particular smile which subordinates have when they are already certain their trifle will be granted.

"What are you thinking, Atila? She never worked as a secretary for me."

Atila bent over in embarrassment and asked for an exception to be made.

"That would not be proper," said the manufacturer and looked indignantly away because he had been bothered with something so petty.

"Just let me telephone," Atila said outside to Anna. "I will let them have the information they need."

Anna brought the message to the new firm but the chief clerk, Mr. Raven, insisted on proceeding properly. The boss was away and on his return their affairs had to be presented in an orderly manner.

And suddenly the phrase "secretarial experience" took on enormous proportions in Anna's mind. This tiny phrase which meant nothing, a mockery of language, a falsely applied concept, it became her fate. Anna thought of her mother's face and went to look for the boss one more time. How should you know what this job means for me? Misfortune does not dare to take a single step towards you, she was going to say.

The foreman, Mr. Atila, met her on the corridor and nodded to her. When he found out, however, that she was going over his head, he adopted that offended expression which schoolmasters make at their pupils after they have taken their *Matura* and graduated from school, as if to say, are they still going to greet me in the proper way? Anna ducked her head and humbled herself. She did not have to wait. The servant came back directly. She had not gained admittance.

Anna thought of the moment when she would come home and everyone would look at her, and she searched her memory for someone who was good and could help, and she remembered Mr. Pot, co-director of the firm Gold & Pot, who always gave her a jovial slap on the back whenever he came into the factory. Even though Mr. Pot did not buy from Salzman, he only sold, Pot had been of assistance to him in recent times smuggling foreign currency, and the manufacturer was in his debt. When he came in with Anna, the boss was busy taking the temperature of his champion greyhound. To begin the beast turned his head away in reluctance, but then gave in. Siegfried Salzman did not respond to Anna's shy greeting.

"Miss Seidler did not work as a secretary with me," he then said in a loud voice.

"Make a leetle exception," Pot intoned, making no effort to tone down his Yiddish dialect. He had no tact whatsoever and did not understand how to raise himself up to the manufacturer's level.[4] "You do something for her, what does it cost you, my friend? Just a word, a silly word, I say. It costs you a word and it costs her her position! Where does she get another position in times like these?"

"I make no exceptions!" Siegfried Salzman raised his voice in anger. "And, incidentally, I do not understand you. You are a businessman and must know that a businessman does not put down untruths on paper. That is not correct." He leaned back correctly in his chair.

"What do you mean by correct? Didn't we do those deals with the currency?" Pot winked and pointed to his collar in which the currency had been transported.

That's how Anna's fate was sealed. Siegfried Salzman was reminded of his dignity and advised Mr. Pot to sell his thread somewhere else in future. He looked around the room and the head clerk, the chief executive, his younger brother who was dependent on him, and the typist all nodded their approval to him, and he leaned back like a victor.

Once outside Pot said to Anna, "That's what you get from being nice, is this what I needed?" He let out a sigh and did not want to pay her tram fare because of the mishap and left her standing at the gates.

Suddenly, she felt cold in the threadbare little coat which she had worn for so many winters. She walked slowly over the empty snow-covered ground which separated the factory from the city. Heavy snowflakes fell on her face, and she walked on and waited for a voice to call her from behind. She walked more and more slowly, but the voice did not call out. She waited for another human being to walk past her and cast a look at her, but the piece of ground was empty. She thought of her mother, but there was no longer that warmth in her mother's expression. Her mother now looked fearful, and her father never raised his head but spooned his soup sorrowfully into his mouth. The younger brothers and sisters had old faces because they knew much too much for their years.

The next morning a worker found the young girl dead in the snow. She had closed her eyes and the sorrow had disappeared from her expression. He carried her in his arms into the factory. Then it happened that the girl's pulled-back hair came loose and fell to the ground and it was remarkable that it fell as if from a living body. He looked at the girl's young figure and her heavy hair and thought regretfully how she could have caught his fancy.[5]

The manufacturer Siegfried Salzman was walking down the corridor and wondered what the gathering of people could mean. He stopped a girl and was told the reason. He went up to the small group, but the workers, who usually greeted him humbly, turned their backs on him. Siegfried Salzman looked sharply at each of their faces. He then made a mental note of who to dismiss the next time.

Notes

1. "Der Sieger" by Veza Magd, first published 29 June 1932 in the *Arbeiter-Zeitung*. Reprinted in *Geduld bringt Rosen* (Munich/Vienna: Hanser, 1992).

2. In Goethe's *The Sufferings of Young Werther* (1774), Lotte is cutting bread for six of her younger siblings, aged betwen two and eleven years old, when Werther first sees her. He describes it as "the most charming scene." She explains that she had almost forgotten to give them their tea "and they do not want to have their bread cut by anybody else but me."

3. Unemployment was the most serious economic consequence of the worldwide Depression, set in motion by the Wall Street Crash on the New York Stock Exchange in October 1929. The *Arbeiter-Zeitung* reports

in June 1932 that there were 5.6 million unemployed in Germany, an increase of 1.4 million since June 1931. The proportions for Austria were similar.

4. Salzman's irritation with Topf's Yiddish inflections reveals him too to be Jewish. German-speaking Jews who wanted to stress their allegiance to Germanic culture often chose Wagnerian names such as Siegfried for their children. Atila (Etzel) was less common but served the same purpose. In 1936 seventy percent of those involved in the Viennese textile industry were Jewish. Bruce F. Pauley, "Political Antisemitism in Interwar Vienna," in Ivar Oxaal, Michael Pollak, and Gerhard Botz (eds.), *Jews, Antisemitism and Culture in Vienna* (London/New York: Routledge and Kegan Paul, 1987), pp. 152-73, here p. 155. Fritz Rosenfeld in the *Arbeiter-Zeitung* of 30 March 1932 had entitled his review of the film "Jung-Siegfried 1932," which perhaps also inspired Canetti's choice of name for her triumphant villain. Rosenfeld sees the involvement of such figures as Leonhard Frank, who wrote the screenplay, as evidence of the sad decline (a *Götterdämmerung* no less) of the UfA, Germany's once proud film studios. Albers is a new Siegfried because of the way he masters his own fate, just as the Nibelungen hero, immortalized for UfA by Fritz Lang, overcame the dragon and successfully wooed Brünhilde on his king's behalf.

5. It is cruelly ironic that the first man to recognize Anna's physical attractiveness does so only after she is dead. Canetti often remarks on her characters' eyes and the ways they use them, or do not use them, to look at the world and their fellow human beings. Put crudely, bad characters see what they want to see, while the good can see the truth. In "Clairvoyants" she makes a distinction between "*Hell*seher" (its German title) and "*Falsch*seher," that is between those who see clearly and those who see wrongly. In "The Victor" her recognition of men's failure to see Anna in her true beauty belongs to the story's accusatory sexual politics.

Patience Brings Roses[1]

When the Prokops left Russia, they hid their jewelery in the following way.[2] Bobby, the son, carried a hollowed-out stick, which was fat just as he was. Into the hollowed-out inside went the emeralds, rubies, and immaculate diamonds. The handle on Mrs. Prokops' umbrella was in the shape of a little dog with a ruff. Inside his head rested two pairs of earrings. Tamara, the daughter, carried a gentleman's umbrella. A necklace was coiled up inside its handle. The meat-carving knife was clapped shut in its wide casing, which concealed a fortune. Only Ljubka, the orphan, had nothing with her. Next to her lay the provisions, and Mrs. Prokop also entrusted the little white breadrolls into her safekeeping.

The customs officers did not find anything in particular.
So animated did Mrs. Prokop suddenly become after their examination that her fellow passengers suddenly noticed what a beautiful woman she still was despite her years. Her full, tall figure quivered. She looked well cared for. But the care that went into her grooming was not that of someone who took a bath each day and laid great store on clothes which smelled good. No, her rounded, pink cheeks showed that each day of her life she had slept until she was no longer tired, and, as she always knew where her next meal would be coming from, that she had never had to eat until she was full.

In what would have been less than an hour's walk from the Russian border, Mrs. Prokop took the bag containing the rolls from her niece. She hurriedly broke one open and, her nostrils quivering with greed, plucked a ring from its inside, a ring with diamonds the size of hazelnuts. Everyone looked in amazement at the ring. Ljubka blanched. "But auntie, they can execute you for that!"

"God looks after the innocent," Mrs. Prokop said, pointed towards God, who was apparently enthroned on the luggage rack, and, broke off a piece of the roll, which she passed to Ljubka. Then she opened up each roll one after the other and filled her pockets with jewels.

Ljubka did not say a word more but got up and hid in the corridor. She cried because she feared the fate which she had just escaped, and perhaps she cried too because she had no parents and no one at all who protected her: the only people responsible for her protection had just brought her into mortal danger and thought nothing whatsoever of it.

Tamara was meanwhile looking with one eye out of the window to check that they really had crossed over the border and with the other into the corridor to make sure the customs officers were not still on the prowl. Her gaze finally rested on the sumptuous jewelery which was piling up, and she said nervously, "Stop it please, Mama."

The contrast between her voice and her face was so startling that the other passengers looked up when she said this. They had just been thinking how she resembled the Tzarina's sister, and when Tamara fell silent again they again felt inclined to admire her fine features. At that point, the first station after the border was called out.

Mrs. Prokop now took out a large, sparkling diamond ring from her bag and passed it meaningfully to her daughter, giving the other passengers a fright because Tamara laughed.

How that fine face was now contorted! Rough lines, bare gums, wrinkles which reached as far as her temples, and then her ears – it was her ears which drew one's attention more than anything else. They were like a dog's when you pull back his flaps, twisted, brown sockets, and her whole laugh betrayed no sign of joy, but just a meanness which could not be hidden. It was not difficult to guess what Tamara was mean about.

The laugh disappeared suddenly from her face and the other passengers felt relieved. When they got out at the next station, Mrs. Prokop began to empty Bobby's stick. All the jewelery now went into a little bag she was holding out and did not let go of for a single minute.

From Karlsbad the family travelled to Vienna. Here they bought a five-room apartment which they had redesigned by a modern architect, built-in furniture, central heating, an electric water heater for the bath, lighting as bright as day with layered shades. Tamara loved explaining their luxuries to guests. "It is quite impossible to ruin your eyes," she said each time about the layered shades. It was only the wallpaper which caused mother and daughter to quarrel. Mrs. Prokop's late husband owned two factories before the Revolution (when they were confiscated he died of a stroke), and Mrs. Prokop could not get used to the idea of not having these two factories. She ordered Salubra wallhangings, but Tamara put her foot down.[3] She cancelled the Salubra wallpaper because you could not take it with you when you moved out. She had the walls painted, imitation silk, and that cost quite enough.

Tamara would not tolerate a housemaid. A housemaid was a danger on account of the expensive jewelery, the furs, and currency in the apartment, she would explain to astounded guests. The hard work was done by Ljubka. But Tamara was not lazy either, she cooked, scrubbed, was not too proud to clean the floor, and looked after her mother, who often suffered from hypochondria: she was too young for her age. That was her illness.

The very same Tamara appeared in the evenings at parties, wrapped in mink and flattered by gentlemen (mink coats are not two a penny), and only her hands had a rough shine. Her skin made one think of chicken's feet and her nails were bent, but nobody noticed that.

Being so busy and such a success it is no wonder that Tamara had the last word at home and took over the role of the father. And she persuaded Mrs. Prokop to stop letting her son steal the shirt from off her back. Whenever Bobby came home with gambling debts, Tamara pointed with her long, bony finger at the five newly renovated rooms and said: "Do you want to sink any lower?" Mrs. Prokop did not want to sink any lower. Bobby was given a once-only sum as start-up capital and was made to accept that he had to do some work. His work, conducted on a purely private basis, bound neither by an alarm clock nor the taxman, consisted of selling items of jewelery to his acquaintances, and fortune smiled on him since they thought of him as a fine fellow.

He did not, of course, carry the jewels to the customer himself. He merely went down to the caretaker, who had to take care of that too. After a while, however, these errands began to be a nuisance to the caretaker, as in a house with forty apartments (twenty-five of which were occupied by finer folk), one two-schilling piece more or less made little difference to him.

He therefore made his excuses one day and drew the young gentleman's attention to the absolutely reliable company messenger Littlemouse, who lived in a courtyard apartment, which had just a living room, a back room, and a kitchen.[4] Bobby wondered for a moment to himself that there should be courtyard apartments, with living room, box room, kitchen in a house occupied by gentlemen and commanded Mr. Littlemouse to come to him, pointing down as he did so with his index finger at the spot directly in front of his feet. When he took the solitaire which the customer had ordered out of his bag, he had some second thoughts – it was six carats. But these second thoughts disappeared the moment Mr. Littlemouse stood before him. Bobby cast his eye over his worn-out grey coat, his torn shirt, poor but clean, and without another thought at all he handed over the solitaire and the address, without even insisting on a confirmation of receipt. Company messenger Littlemouse felt so honored by this trust that he would have preferred to run the errand for nothing. When he also was given a two-schilling piece for his troubles and the young gentleman threw the receipt, which he had brought back for the sake of propriety, back in his face, Mr. Littlemouse saw that a new era in his life had dawned.

And he was not wrong. He could count on the extra earnings, which honored him so much, at least three times a month, and the young gentleman was not stingy. If he found a crumpled fiver in his pocket, then Mr. Littlemouse got the fiver, and it did not matter at all if it was torn, as he could stick it back together with paper left over from a sheet of stamps and cash it in for five shiny silver coins. The receipts which he brought back from each errand piled up in a cupboard at home. He did not tire of keeping them.

The money which was spent on these errands annoyed Tamara considerably. Either her brother should go himself or he should ask Ljubka. But this time her protestations to their mother had no effect. Mrs. Prokop had always favored manners becoming of an aristocrat. She secretly handed out tips and small presents (she liked having protégés), and Bobby himself found having a servant more appropriate to his own sense of what he was worth. His sister did not think she was doing any harm if in her anger, meeting the messenger by chance on the staircase, she burdened him with an errand of her own, for which he received no reward. Doing this did not give her the right sense of satisfaction. At home she had Ljubka, but nevertheless this way Ljubka was worn out less quickly and could be used for other purposes. Mr. Littlemouse discharged his debt of gratitude, for he felt himself in Bobby's debt, immeasurably in his debt.

For a long time the Prokops could afford to lead a comfortable life, but one day there came serious discord. The Prokops' luxurious, satisfied life was suddenly disturbed because of a fall in the value of the pound. It was not only that the pound fell: all the other currencies into which the Prokops had transformed their jewelery became unsafe. One day they realized that they had lost one-third of their fortune and it was on this very day that Bobby came home in an agitated state, which was not like him at all, and confessed that he had a gambling debt and would be dishonored if he did not pay it.

Tamara then stood up. She stood up and explained that she had had enough. Tamara was not only the pillar by day and a glamorous apparition by night, she had also recently become engaged to an extremely rich attorney twenty years her senior, and on this occasion all Bobby could manage to do was to make Mrs. Prokop more anxious and go to bed moaning. More than that he could not for the life of him manage to achieve, for which reason he was obliged to debase himself. He had to debase himself to the extent of handing over the rest of his jewelery to a servant to take to the Dorotheum. Indeed, he even had to lie in wait for the right moment to remove a fur from the premises, a sealskin coat, which his mother rarely wore.[5] All this brought him no more than four thousand schillings and he needed five thousand. He called up his customers one by one and asked them all to pay their installments one day earlier (customers nowadays do not buy in cash), but they laughed back unpleasantly down the line. They had, on the contrary, been wanting to ask him for a postponement. In a bad mood, he walked through the five rooms with built-in furniture and was annoyed for the first time by the modern unfussiness because there was nothing of any significance he could take away without it being noticed. And now Bobby had to decide to ask his friends, the Seiferts, for cash (embarrassing because he liked to show off in their company) and to wait until the atmosphere at home calmed down.

In a foul temper he went down the staircase in his fur and

walked across the lobby to the apartment of company messenger Littlemouse.

Company messenger Littlemouse lived with his wife and two children on the ground floor. From the lobby, you walked straight into the kitchen and saw the furniture that stood there, which through much scrubbing gleamed as if it were painted white. The living room, which opened onto the yard, was large and kept terribly clean. Mr. Littlemouse, his wife, and his little daughter Steffi slept in the twin matrimonial beds. Steffi, a very small twelve-year-old girl, had golden-red hair, which would have turned any moderately pretty girl into a beauty. In Steffi's case, it just crowned her ugliness. It seemed that all aspects of ugliness had resolved to land on Steffi. Her nose consisted of wide holes, and her mouth was an even wider continuation of it. Her eyes could not be made out at all. You could see two tiny red brown dots, but nothing twinkled, nothing looked out, there was nothing which made a sound or had an opinion. Instead of a complexion she had freckles. And yet Mr. and Mrs. Littlemouse gazed in wonderment at their daughter, in wonderment at her straight figure, her nimble little legs, her dainty little hands and feet. They admired Steffi, admired her so much, that in all her life the little girl had never had any suspicion that she was ugly.

The explanation for their admiration could in part be found in their first child, their little son. Little son is not the right term. What lay on the sofa had hands. But they were the only features the creature had in common with a human being. Instead of legs he had two lifeless rods, as scrawny as a skeleton, a broad box instead of a chest, a bald head where he should have had hair, and black stumps in place of teeth. A dark fur covered other parts of his body. He babbled rather than spoke, and in a way only the Littlemouses could understand. He was animated not by thoughts but by fleeting impressions, which could move him to sudden bursts of anger or joy. This insignificant collection of characteristics was known to the world of medicine as "Small." He had got "Small," Mr. Littlemouse used to say to the doctors when he brought the lad to the clinic. They immediately made the sign of the cross over him, but let the ailing man carry the heavy child to the clinic each day so that they could demonstrate how he could not be cured.

Company messenger Littlemouse, often known as Little

Mousy after his wife had once called him that, Mr. Little Mousy brought home thirty schillings in wages every week and handed them over to his wife. It was enough for their simple fare and the rent, for their smallest room was rented. Even though Mrs. Littlemouse did not possess a hat and she wore the same yellowish-brown coat in winter and summer, she and her husband did not ask for more in life. They did not ask for it because noone took the trouble to enlighten them that fate does not suffer those who are satisfied with their lot. Fate takes and takes until it gets to the last thread of clothing off the back of the contented. Only then does it relent. The ambitious, on the other hand, take the battle to the enemy themselves and the less scrupulous their means, the stronger they become.

Bobby Prokop was just such a valiant battler. If I don't wear a fur then I freeze, and if I do not eat well then I am in a bad mood, and if I am in a bad mood then I don't do any business. So Bobby wore a fur, dined at the Hotel Sacher, and was always in fine spirits.[6]

Until today. Today he needed five thousand and he only had four thousand. He had to clear his debt; otherwise, he was finished at the Diamond Club, and that meant he was as good as finished in society, finished in business circles, finished in the world.

His knock on the door of company messenger Littlemouse was brutal.

It absolutely has to be said that Mr. and Mrs. Littlemouse possessed a very special, conspicuous characteristic: they were stupid. Whoever could tell by looking recognized it in the deformed shape of their head, their surprised, tiny eyes, and their long horse-like faces (they looked alike), and whoever could not tell by looking, recognized it when one of them spoke. Mrs. Littlemouse's characteristic phrase was: "Do you understand?," and she would show enormous surprise if one had understood, for instance, that it was hotter in the sun than in the shade. Mr. Littlemouse was a degree less stupid and used to explain everything to people in advance, in order to make up for their lack of comprehension, for which Mrs. Littlemouse admired him boundlessly. His phrase was "for the simple reason" or "why then," which would be accompanied by an explanation.

His stupidity was recognized by everybody and not least by

his boss, because out of his sixty employees he chose the one who was the worst paid to entrust with the wages for all the workers in the factory, which Mr. Littlemouse had delivered on time every month for the last twenty-five years.

Bobby had noticed the stupidity of this man straightaway and used to speak to him in telegram style.

"Must come here!" he commanded when Mrs. Littlemouse opened the door. His words sounded violent, in spite of his quiet voice which was cushioned by fat.

"For exceptional reasons that will not be possible today," Mr. Littlemouse said from inside and did not come out. His voice sounded dried up, like a door that was creaking on its hinges.

"Why?" called Bobby impatiently.

"You see," said Mrs. Littlemouse quietly, "he has brought the money for the factory home. He never stirs from the room when the money is inside. Do you understand?"

"What money's that?" Bobby's guttural voice grew soft.

"The money for the factory," she whispered reverently.

Bobby guided his elegant fur through their meager kitchen and even had to suffer the sight of the idiot. He was sitting up on the couch grunting with pleasure and making crazy expressions, delighted by the fat gentleman in the fur, by the smell of pomade, eau de cologne, and Coty Parfum which was quite unfamiliar to him and gave the room a whiff of wealth and good fortune. The red-haired girl stood quivering in a corner. She quivered in excitement at the sight of the posh gentleman.

"Why can't you run the errand?"

"For exceptional reasons I unfortunately cannot go out today," Mr. Littlemouse said, "because I have to stay at home."

"And why?"

"For the simple reason," Mr. Littlemouse said, "because he has got the money in the box," his wife interrupted him.

"What money?"

"The money that I have to bring to the factory at five o'clock tomorrow morning." Mr. Littlemouse's eyelids trembled because he was ashamed by his inability to be of service.

"What a nuisance." Bobby fell rather heavily into the armchair. He breathed wearily. "You see, I need you urgently." The corners of his mouth stood out from his fat feminine face. They were suddenly astoundingly energetic.

"I am really very sorry," Mr. Littlemouse asserted and his eyelids carried on trembling, looking as if he wanted to cry, "but I am not allowed to stir from the spot. Why then? My wife is alone with the children. Burglars can come and steal the money away."

"How much is it then?"

"Thirty thousand schillings," said Mr. Littlemouse in a dignified voice.

"That gives me an idea. If you don't want to run the errand for me and are not taking the money into the factory until tomorrow morning, then you can lend me one thousand schillings, which I need urgently now. I have left it at a friend's house, where I wanted to send you now. I will bring the money back to you by the end of the evening. You will get it in three to four hours."

"But I can't do that." Mr. Littlemouse laughed at the young gentleman's naivety.

"Why not?"

"For the simple reason that it does not belong to me."

"But I am just borrowing it! Just for a couple of hours! Nobody will know anything about it, or don't you trust me?"

Mr. Littlemouse was deeply offended. He strained his small head, which looked as if it had been cut off with a knife, in order to make himself understood. He looked as if he wanted to cry. Then he had a flash of inspiration.

"I cannot give you the money, young sir, for the simple reason that I cannot take it out. The envelope is sealed."

"Show it to me!"

Glad of the opportunity to justify himself, Littlemouse hurried to the cupboard, took two keys out of his breastpocket, unlocked the cupboard, unlocked a trunk, and took out a large, fat envelope. It was sealed tight.

"That can be opened."

"That's not allowed. It's not allowed to tear it open!" Mr. Littlemouse sounded as nervous as a schoolboy.

"Who's talking about tearing? That can be opened and re-sealed without making a tear!"

Mrs. Littlemouse was dumbfounded. "How can that be done?"

Mr. Littlemouse reached for the envelope.

"Don't be afraid," Bobby said, offended, taking out a pencil. "See," he looked genially to Mrs. Littlemouse and pulled the pencil slowly through the parts which were stuck together. The seal itself came unstuck without any damage being done. The money, big bundles of one hundred and one thousand schilling bills, was revealed to them. Mrs. Littlemouse's eyes popped out of her head. But not at the large amounts of money. That made no impression on her because it was not hers. She was amazed that a letter could be opened without making a tear.

Bobby's nostrils heaved. "You must seal it up again straight away, young sir!" The skin around Mr. Littlemouse's eyes tightened, as if he were a baby about to cry.

"See," he bent the envelope open and took out the bills. "I am borrowing fifteen hundred schillings." Bobby had decided to gamble with the other five hundred, to win, and to pay back the money before the night was over.

"Your money is safe!"

"But I have to be on the train tomorrow at five o'clock in the morning. I have to go to the factory. I cannot give you the money, young sir."

"Don't be worried. You'll get to the factory. To calm you down, I will bring it back tonight. Hold on to this." He pointed to the envelope with the money, and Mrs. Littlemouse put it obediently in the trunk. "Nobody will know anything about it, understand. I will not breathe a word and neither will you and you will get your money, no mistake." Bobby lifted himself and his heavy fur up from the chair and from an upright position waved at Mr. Littlemouse, who was scared to death, at Mrs. Littlemouse, who was laughing as if nothing had happened, at the idiot, who was whooping with joy, and the only person he overlooked was the girl who was quivering in the corner.

After the door had closed behind him, Mr. Littlemouse for the first time in his life had a thought which would not have discredited a less stupid person. He said to himself that he would not get the money. Nevertheless, he sat up the whole night and waited. He waited and the baby-like wrinkles on his forehead grew deeper until at the depth of his misery something occurred to him which cheered him a little. It occurred to him that he was innocent, that he had not got his hands dirty, and that nothing could happen to him.

"Mr. Mousy, lie down and go to sleep." He did not move. He listened for steps in the corridor, looked at the clock, at the twilight outside and waited. At four in the morning, he took out the envelope and examined it. He stuck it together. It jumped back open. He mixed some glue and spread some on the edges. At half past four, he set off for the station. This time he did not carry the bag as carefully as he had in all the previous months in the last twenty-five years; he carried it as if what was in it was worth nothing any more, as if twenty-eight thousand, eight-hundred schillings had no value.

At the factory they gave Littlemouse the receipt without hesitation, but instead of taking it to work, he went back home straightaway. He ate nothing and he did not answer his wife's question. After the meal he took his hat and coat and went to the front entrance of the house and climbed up the steps to the apartments where the finer people lived. He knocked shyly at the Prokops' door and demanded to speak to the young gentleman.

"He is not at home," said Ljubka.

"But I have to speak to him." Mr. Littlemouse obviously did not understand that this was simply not possible.

"He has not come home since yesterday," Ljubka explained kindly.

"But I have to speak to him," Mr. Littlemouse insisted obstinately, "because I have to deliver the money. If I don't deliver the money I will lose my job."

"What money?" a hard voice enquired.

"The money that the young gentleman borrowed from my boss."

Mr. Littlemouse always used to think in such polite formulations.

"He is not here," said Tamara brusquely and shut the door in his face.

Mr. Littlemouse still did not go to the office but back to his living room overlooking the yard, where he sat down without saying a word and waited.

Meanwhile, this is what had happened to Bobby. He had gone to the club, and as he deposited his fur in the cloakroom and threw down his gloves for the attendant, the younger club members were talking about him and placing bets on whether or not he would come. "He's not coming," said a fellow player, the same one he owed the money to. At exactly this moment, Bobby opened the door with his fat fingers, squeezed his opulent body through it, and with reddened cheeks and some reticence greeted the assembled company. He was in no hurry as he wanted to enjoy the tension, and he exchanged pleasantries. When Mr. Ranzberg, the distinguished man of commerce, and Mr. Wolf, his distinguished colleague from the City Hall, went past, Bobby reached into his briefcase, as if he had forgotten something, made a bow to the two gentlemen, and nonchalantly laid down the money in front of his fellow player, laid it down as if he had taken offence, as if the latter had doubted Bobby's influence, honor, and wealth. Then he turned to the two distinguished gentlemen, who were talking to him in an extremely friendly manner, and when they had gone, Bobby's happy playing partner suggested a game. "I absolutely have to get my revenge," thought Bobby, and the others thought so too. And now the corners of Bobby's mouth became astoundingly soft, the whole of his fat face became one round mass of flesh, not dissimilar to that part of his body on which he was sitting; he always looked like that when he had decided on something, which he only did resolutely if his decision favored his comforts. With his soft face he nodded with a laugh to his briefcase, pointed out its sad condition, and he could do so with his honor intact, for who can lay five thousand on the table in cash at the end of the month? All those assembled honored it too, not least his happy playing partner, who had immediately put away his five thousand, but now more or less forced Bobby to take back a thousand. Bobby pictured himself replacing the money in the damaged envelope, saw the money in his own pocket too, and he pictured it all the more clearly because he knew very well that the disgrace would fall on him if it was missing. Only the room belonging to the company messenger was unfortunately a dark hole, the man a poor devil, and Bobby found himself in a dazzlingly lit room with burgundy-red padded walls, and who should approach him but Count d'Evil, who invited him with an elegant bow to a table. Bobby held one thousand schillings in his hand, thought of all that money at home, a third of which as good as belonged to him, the foreign currency, jewelery, furs. He thought of his reputation. He dissolved in awe in front of his highness and agreed to go gambling ...

He did not win and was in a bad mood. He could not at any price now try to touch anyone for money. That would have been too pitiful a sight. The Count then suggested a bar. Bobby went along with the rest. Somewhat reluctantly he latched on to the ones with money in their pockets, as without them he was truly lost. In the bar after a few drinks, he got very merry and confident and celebrated his joy with another drink. Everything around him was glistening, and when he woke up it was the next morning and he was lying in the unfamiliar surroundings of an apartment belonging to an ultra fashionable young lady of the demi-monde and he found that he was in company. The whole crowd from the bar was rolling around on dissolute piles of bedding, armchairs, rugs. Bobby himself lay on the floor, next to rather than on top of a heap of cushions.

They went as they were to the Diana Swimming Pool to get rid of the hangover, and then they dined at Zykan's.[7] Bobby more than once began to pluck up the courage to touch his playing partner for money, but he felt so hung over that he did not get as far as saying a single word.

Refreshed by an excellent dinner at Zykan's, surrounded by elegant company, loved and respected by one and all, Bobby was not able to imagine that he should reproach himself for borrowing for a day some money which he was going to pay back anyway. He stayed with his friends until late at night and returned home firmly resolved to sort out the matter by confessing everything secretly to his mother in the morning. He still, by the way, had six hundred schillings in his pocket. Things were not as bad as all that.

Mr. Littlemouse had in the meantime stayed quietly at home and waited. He waited for it to come and it came. It came in the shape of an employee of the firm who was one grade higher than him. Mr. Clearout came through the door, saw the poor accommodation, and knew immediately that Littlemouse had taken the money, as how could anyone who was so poor not steal? So, he went up to him and said:

"Do you know that money is missing in the factory?"

"Yes, I know that," said Mr. Littlemouse.

"Ah, well there we have it!" The employee took a step back. "Have you taken the money?"

"No, I have not taken the money."

"How do you know then that it is missing?" he asked cleverly and wetted his lower lip.

"I know that it is missing, but I didn't take it."

"Come with me for a moment, Mr. Littlemouse."

Mr. Clearout considered the meager apartment one more time, the bare room, the woefully appointed kitchen, the door to the lobby which was hanging off its hinges, and thought of his brother who had been unemployed for two years and who he would recommend.

The boss of the carriage rental company did not believe for one moment that the money had been embezzled and did not even make enquiries when Littlemouse did not come in the morning with the receipt. He must be ill, said the chief clerk, and a few employees within earshot nodded. Later a telephone call was made from the factory, and even then the boss asked if they had not made a mistake. The receiver was gently replaced and an investigation started. It produced an envelope which had been tampered with and pencil marks. The boss immediately sent someone to the apartment of his company messenger.

As Littlemouse entered, the boss was bending over four different drafts which he had to compare with one another: number one, section A, section B, section C, and so forth. He was just pausing at one, section C. With the fingers of his left hand, he pointed to the relevant section on draft numbers one and two, with the right hand he held a pencil on section c of draft number three. He had to search for the corresponding places in draft number four with his eye, and that made him anxious. Littlemouse was standing there for a while before the boss noticed him. Then he looked up.

At the sight of his honest equine features and his stupid eyes the boss knew immediately that his old servant Littlemouse had not taken the money.

"He knows that it's missing, but he hasn't taken it," said Mr. Clearout with a Jesuitic smile.

"Certainly I haven't taken it," Mr. Littlemouse insisted with some annoyance.

"You did not take the money?"

"No, I did not take the money."

"Are you aware that it is missing? Quickly!"

"Yes, certainly I am aware that it is missing, I saw myself how the young gentleman took it out."

"Which young gentleman? Quickly!"

"The young gentleman who came into my apartment."

"Is your wife a servant? Tell us quickly!"

"No, my wife is not a servant. Why then? Engelbert has to lie down all day, and when he is on his own, he goes berserk. What can I do when the other tenants complain to the owner? He is in other respects a very clever child but he sometimes gets impatient because he is lame ..."

"But who took the money? Quickly, quickly! What's his name?"

"I can't say what he is called."

"Well, don't you know?"

"I know but I can't say for the simple reason that it would be unpleasant for the young man."

This made the boss forget to hold the pencil over section C. "What? Are you out of your mind? You will lose your job. I will have you locked up."

"Sir, I have really not taken the money." His tiny eyes peered out in dread.

"Well, *tell* us then *who* did."

"I cannot tell you that for the simple reason I have already said."

"You are dismissed." The boss was very annoyed because he had now lost all his sections and had to start again at the beginning.

"I have really not taken the money."

"Go." Littlemouse was led out.

He went home, ate nothing for his evening meal, and let himself be persuaded by his wife to sleep for a while. "Tomorrow the young gentleman will bring the money and everything will be all right. Do you understand, Mr. Mousy?"

Mr. Mousy lay himself down and waited humbly until he fell asleep. The next morning he woke up late. No sooner was he washed and dressed than the young gentleman really did appear. He had color in his cheeks and was in a good mood.

"I have been dismissed, young sir."

"Whatever for?"

"Because the money was missing."

"But you are going to give it back," said Bobby irritably and pushed out the corners of his mouth. "I have brought it with me."

"It is too late, I have been dismissed."

"Did you say that I had taken the money?"

"No, I didn't say that, why then? It would have been unpleasant for you if I had said your name."

"You needn't have worried. You could have said my name, then you wouldn't have been dismissed. That was not clever of you." Bobby made a stern expression. "There is no point in doing so now, however; don't say anything about me now. We would only have more bother from it. Here are five hundred schillings. I will bring you the rest after lunch. You bring them the money and everything will be all right."

"That won't do any good, young sir. I have been dismissed. They have already got someone else."

"Ridiculous! They have to take you back. What did they used to pay you, by the way?"

"One hundred and twenty schillings."

"One hundred and twenty schillings a week – that's not much."

"One hundred and twenty schillings a month!"

"One hundred and twenty schillings a month!" Bobby was genuinely astonished. "It's a lucky thing you got dismissed. One hundred and twenty schillings! How long have you been working for the company?"

"Twenty-five years."

"And you only get a hundred and twenty schillings a month. With your abilities you should be earning four times that. You will be too! Don't let yourself be talked into anything by your boss, even if he does want to take you back. One hundred and twenty schillings with your abilities!"

"Have you understood, Mr. Mousy? You should get more. Look at his handwriting, young sir."

"Exactly! His handwriting. If you had shown me this handwriting last week, I would have got you a position in a bank. But you don't need that. Write applications – you will get a brilliant job, ten jobs!"

Littlemouse looked at him in bewilderment. For twenty-five years this thought had not occurred to him *once*. One hundred and twenty schillings after twenty-five years was really not very much. If he got a reference, he could improve his situation significantly. The prospect exhilarated him.

"Do you understand, Mr. Mousy?" She laughed happily and Littlemouse went directly to the office and let the boss know he was there.

"Here are five hundred schillings, and after lunch I will bring you the rest."

"He's paying me damages," thought the boss to himself, so he did take the money after all.

But when Littlemouse really did bring the thousand schillings in the afternoon, he had his doubts once more.

"Well, now you can tell me who took the money, Littlemouse," the boss said with a trace of benevolence.

"Unfortunately I cannot say that," Littlemouse insisted, "for the simple reason that the young gentleman is my benefactor."

"Do you know it's a criminal offence? I can have you locked up."

Littlemouse kept humbly silent.

"It will cost you your job." The boss locked the thousand schilling note in his drawer. "Take your wages and go."

"Sir, I would like to ask sir for a reference," Mr. Littlemouse said to the boss's amazement, with the most satisfied expression in the world.

"You will get a reference and a full month's wages. Have you already got a new job then?"

"As good as in the bag," said Littlemouse happily.

The new company messenger, Mr. Clearout, the brother of the employee just above him, accompanied Mr. Littlemouse with excessive enthusiasm down the stairs, glad that he was not making any trouble.

The young gentleman paid a visit to Littlemouse that very same evening. The young gentleman brought him one hundred schillings. "Here is your start-up capital. Not that you have any expenses. Just write applications."

"And they paid us the wages for the whole month," said Mrs. Littlemouse excitedly.

"Then you can live it up!" Bobby was very pleased that they were not making any demands on him. And then he left, forgetting the Littlemouse family the moment he went out of the door.

An important time began for Littlemouse. Every day promptly in the morning, he sat himself down with a newspaper and wrote applications like a man possessed. He wrote until midday, took them himself to the administrative department to save stamps, wrote, admired by his wife, full of self-admiration for what he was doing, and never got a reply.

His friends from the savings club put in a word for him, as did the neighbors in the other apartments overlooking the courtyard and an employee of the carriage rental company, whom he paid a visit, but he did not get a job. He did not dare to go to see his former boss, and that was just as well. For the boss needed sixty workers and not a single one more. So they took the gold clock, which Mrs. Littlemouse had inherited from her sister, to the Dorotheum, then their silver wedding beaker, then Mr. Littlemouse's winter coat – the weather had turned warm already, then their good tablecloth, then their bed linen, and then they had nothing left, and they began to get into debt at the grocer's and the baker's until they could no longer go shopping in the neighborhood and Mrs. Littlemouse had to walk several streets to get bread and potatoes. And at precisely this point the young gentleman stopped asking him to run errands.

One day as his wife and children were sleeping, Mr. Littlemouse looked at the bare room, the uncovered mattresses he was lying on, the torn blanket which covered up his crippled son, the unshapely head of this child, the enormous leg braces which stood in the corner and had not helped at all, the little girl who cowered next to him, anemic, her stomach contracted, and his wife who still admired him for his abilities and was sleeping deeply and trustingly. He looked at the scene and got up very quietly, went into the kitchen, and locked the room from the outside.

After some time, Mrs. Littlemouse woke up and noticed a coating on her tongue. She looked for her husband and found the bed was empty. She ran to the door of the kitchen – it was bolted. Gas was seaping through the crack. She yanked open the window and screamed for help. The porter came, the neighbors came, the fire engine came. Mr. Littlemouse went to a hospital, and a notice was printed in the newspaper. In contrast to the concise notices on those who had grown tired of life which appeared on a daily basis, this one concluded: "The punctilious cleanliness in the more than meager accommodation was striking."

But Mr. Littlemouse did not die. He caught pneumonia, and when that passed, he was deemed fit to be nursed at home. Meanwhile, his wife had borrowed a machine and was taking in sewing jobs, which she knew how to do.

When people came to check up and saw that sewing was going on here, they withdrew Mr. Littlemouse's unemployment benefit. Mrs. Littlemouse remarked that she would prefer to stop doing the sewing since she earned less than the benefit amounted to. This careless remark was noted down.

Mr. Littlemouse deteriorated rapidly. He lay in bed, coughed and spluttered and spread tuberculosis bacilli over the little daughter who lay next to him. When she began to cough, Mr. Littlemouse was taken to hospital again.

This time he was not allowed out, and that was just as well, as Mrs. Littlemouse had pawned his suit. She worked from five in the morning to twelve at night and only earned enough for bread and potatoes. The neighbors who also had apartments on the ground floor by the courtyard helped out and made angry speeches about the people upstairs who had caused their whole misfortune, but it did not do any good. Who listens to groundfloor apartments? The finer folk in the finer apartments had heard too of the circumstances of the attempted suicide. But because the Littlemouse family were an unpleasant sight and Mr. Bobby in contrast a very pleasant one when he descended the stairs in his elegant clothes and uttered a friendly greeting, because the Prokops owned the most beautiful apartment in the whole of the three-part housing complex, the finer folk said to their maids that the story must have happened rather differently. Everyone knows how rumors come into being, and they greeted Mrs. Prokop especially sympathetically and looked the young gentleman especially kindly in the eyes, the gentleman with a certain complicit solidarity which signified that one would not let oneself be ruined by the proles.

Only once did Mrs. Prokop get a shock. Just as she came back from shopping one day – she liked to go to the delicatessen herself – she saw something horrifying.

Someone had drawn a skull and crossbones on the door to

the apartment with the following threatening verse in explanation:

Take a good look at him, you impertinent rich folks.
Can you show no heart to him till the day he croaks?

Mrs. Prokop took the death's head to be an evil omen, became hysterical and went to bed with a deathly illness. Ljubka had to remove the terrifying drawing immediately and Mrs. Prokop asked her son, who was somewhat reticent, to tell her the whole story one more time.

"That it was you who brought such disgrace upon us is obvious," said Tamara, "but not on account of the cretin. For if a person has what it takes, he can step naked on to the street and will come home in a furcoat with a car, and if he does not have what it takes, he will go to wrack and ruin anyway. The disgrace which you have brought upon us is on account of the letters which Bernhard gets every day."

The letters which Bernhard was getting every day were anonymous letters in which the story of the Prokop and Littlemouse families was told not at all badly, and he was warned of allying himself with them.

Satisfied by the comparison which liberated him from the scruples of his conscience, Bobby stopped worrying about any of the rest of it.

"What more dreadful things can befall me?" Mrs. Prokop wailed in bed.

"The pound is recovering after all," Bobby said between his teeth and looked grumpily out of the window, the corners of his mouth taut.

"And the gold-based bonds."

"But the schilling here has its full value. What are you getting so worked up for?"

"I have lost twelve per cent," Mrs. Prokop moaned.

"You've got dollars."

"You seem to be forgetting that every tenth man in New York is unemployed," replied Tamara brusquely.

"But then you still have the jewelry."

If only he were outside, but he could not get away today – his pockets were empty. He was so annoyed he was spitting poison.

"Shall we get rid of our nest egg too?" hissed Tamara.

In bed Mrs. Prokop could not forget the skull and

crossbones. She turned to Ljubka who was darning socks next to her. "Off you go, my dear," Mrs. Prokop's tone was always friendly when she spoke to Ljubka. "Take some sugar and flour down to the people." Ljubka knew immediately who she meant. "Give her the keys, child." Tamara gave her the keys but she went with her to see that not too much would be taken out of the house.

With a shopping bag on her arm Ljubka knocked shyly on the Littlemouses' door. The charged atmosphere and arguments upstairs had made her so anxious recently that she was becoming afraid of the family. The red-haired girl answered the door. Ljubka stayed standing shyly at the door. The little girl did not understand why. The door to the room was open. Ljubka saw a dark, bare room – the only dim light came from over the sewing machine in the corner. The idiot lay on the sofa, in the middle of which was a gaping hole.

"Please come in, miss." Mrs. Littlemouse waved with her finger.

"Auntie sends this and would like to know how your husband is," said Ljubka and blushed.

"Very well," said Mrs. Littlemouse kindly. "They are blowing air into him. He will soon get his health back."

"Is that what the doctor said?" asked Ljubka with relief.

"A shopgirl told me. She has been released because she had something on her lung and they blew air into her too and in two years time she got her health back. Do you understand? Please sit down, miss."

Ljubka sat down. She had a dainty but shapely figure and, although her flesh was as soft as pastry dough, her prettiness was appealing. The idiot started to make wild joyful movements.

At that moment the door to the lobby was opened violently. An apprentice boy came in and pompously handed a card to Mrs. Littlemouse. He made as if to go again, but then he noticed the young girl in what in his eyes were fine clothes. Pretending benevolence, he immediately started to concern himself condescendingly with the cripple, patting him jokingly a few times on the cheek. The cripple hit back, half in happiness, half in anger. Meanwhile Mrs. Littlemouse was explaining to Ljubka all the things she would be getting from a charitable institution. "One kilo of *weak* flour," she went through the list, "one kilo of beans, two kilos of potatoes, two packets of malt coffee."

"Wheat flour," the apprentice boy corrected her and stood proudly in front of the girl as if he were the donor himself.

"Isn't that splendid," called out Mrs. Littlemouse, and Ljubka's inhibition and anxiety began to dissolve. It almost seemed as if she was recovering down here in this oppressive poverty from the oppression upstairs among the rich.

The door to the lobby was opened once again without a knock being heard and Mrs. Silk, the neighbor, came in. She went up to the sewing machine and took something she wanted. "I am borrowing your oil can," she said to Mrs. Littlemouse and started to go. But Mrs. Littlemouse held her back and read out the list of donated goods from the charitable institution to her too.

"Well, they have made an effort," said Mrs. Silk, and Mrs. Littlemouse looked at her quite astonished. While they were still talking, the door to the backroom opened and out came a young woman with a bucket. With well-meaning disdain, she gazed on Mrs. Littlemouse, her face drained of color and puffy because of her sedentary lifestyle and the unwholesome fare she lived on. Her disdain was for the stupidity of this woman who worked hard for fifteen hours a day making undergarments and did not even earn as much as she received herself in unemployment benefit.

Ljubka looked with embarrassment at all these people in the room – at the apprentice boy who was taking liberties teasing the idiot, at the tenant who walked through without asking, and at Mrs. Borrower, the neighbor. All these people had one particularity in common. They all moved about the room as if it was not part of Mrs. Littlemouse's apartment. They all behaved as if she were under their jurisdiction. It made Ljubka embarrassed. She got up and Mrs. Littlemouse whispered quickly into her ear that that was the tenant and she paid on time. Then she thanked her warmly and Ljubka left.

From now on, Ljubka spent most of her small allowance at the end of every week to buy something for the Littlemouses. The first time she bought sugar and placed it furtively through the grille from the lobby onto the bench in the kitchen. Then she scurried away. Mrs. Littlemouse saw the packet of sugar, took it down to the caretaker, and explained that the boy from the shop must have delivered it to the wrong address.

"Right you are," Mrs. Unclean, the caretaker, did not even look up. "The right person will come and fetch it soon enough." When nobody had come to fetch the sugar by the end of the week, Mrs. Unclean dipped her own spoon into the big bag and filled up her sugar bowl. At that very moment, Mrs. Littlemouse came down with another packet. This time it contained lentils. "Just leave it there," said Mrs. Unclean graciously, and Mrs. Littlemouse put down the packet on the coal box.

A collection was meanwhile started from among the fourteen neighbors from around the courtyard, and Mrs. Silk gathered up the money.

"Keep it for me," Mrs. Littlemouse asked her. "I could be tempted otherwise. We only eat potato soup now, you see. Do you understand? I have to redeem Mr. Littlemouse's suit because he's coming out of hospital soon."

But Mr. Littlemouse was lying in the hospital ward in a clean bed between snow-white sheets. He was given a good meal four times a day, but he could never enjoy it because he was in great pain. He never went to sleep before midnight, but before five o'clock every morning the red-cheeked nun appeared, showed no mercy, and woke him up. Then his bedsheets were aired and smoothed down, he was given his rubdown, a breakfast, and a thermometer. Afterwards they would have let him go to sleep again, but afterwards he couldn't any more. And every morning before the sister woke him up, Mr. Littlemouse had a vision. In the dark he saw the large, black head belonging to his son, the cripple, he saw his broad ribcage and saw how he came ever closer to him in the dark, how he lay himself down on him, onto his chest, until Mr. Littlemouse had to fight for breath. At that very moment, he would be woken up. "It is really very kind of you to have woken me up," he said each time.

The team of doctors came every morning, twelve doctors led by the consultant, and then Mr. Littlemouse had to sit himself up and breathe in deeply and he would be examined while the consultant explained his case.

"At least that shows that they're examining us thoroughly," Mr. Littlemouse said afterwards to his neighbors in the beds to his left and right and sank back exhausted into his pillows.

They were always complaining about everything. They only showed forbearance to Littlemouse because he distributed his food to them.

Whenever he was in serious pain and the area around his eyes became lined like a tiny baby's, the nun bent stiffly over him, her fat face shining with kindness. "Hurting badly, Mr. Littlemouse?"

He nodded.

One day the twelve doctors came again and the consultant made a sign to him to sit up.

"That unfortunately won't be possible today," Mr. Littlemouse said politely, "for the simple reason ...," and he shut his eyes.

The doctors went on directly to the next bed. All twelve of them and the consultant, and Mr. Littlemouse saw the image of the cripple once again in the dark. Then he felt lighter, as he was too weak now even for the pain, and then he saw his wife's elongated face and the red head of the little girl one more time, and at that point his heart fluttered delicately, and then he was dead.

At the same time, Mrs. Littlemouse was sending the suit into the hospital. An hour later, the hospital servant came through the door. The suit hung over his arm. When Mrs. Littlemouse saw him, she got such a fright that she lost her voice. She looked at the black openings of the sleeves, at the empty collar, at the dangling trouser legs. It was Mr. Littlemouse's empty casing. The little girl started to cry loudly, the idiot bellowed with laughter, Mrs. Littlemouse wrapped her arms around the suit, and the hospital servant laid it over the armchair, with the shoes next to it, also a pocket diary, a pencil, a torn shirt, and Mr. Littlemouse's tie, collar, cuff links, and socks. The hospital servant added a shiny new two-schilling piece, which did not belong to Mr. Littlemouse, but he did not say that. He did not say anything at all and went away as if he were ashamed.

Mrs. Littlemouse went straightaway to visit her dead husband in the hospital, in order to see him one last time, and Steffi had to stay behind with the idiot. When Mrs. Littlemouse came home, wrapped up in a black woolen shawl, her eyes, already weakened by crying, were blinded by the glaring light coming from the first floor of the front part of the building. All the rooms were lit up, whole solar systems were hanging from the ceiling of the five rooms, light bounced off the walls, beams of light. Everyone was beaming – they were celebrating Tamara's engagement.

Mrs. Littlemouse went into the empty apartment, where the empty suit was hanging up, and sat down, impatient for the first time, embittered, desperate. In front of her she saw the burnished red hair belonging to her little girl, who was still bent over the table. Mrs. Littlemouse saw the child and became mildly hopeful once more. She did not hear the knock at the door. Ljubka came in.

Mrs. Prokop, the generous hostess upstairs in the first floor, did not allow the cakes and the plates to be passed round another time when more than three-quarters had already been eaten. New cakes arrived, new giant plates, and what was left over of the fine food was put on a large tray and intended for the Littlemouse family, as Mrs. Prokop loved playing Lady Bountiful. Ljubka carried the tray down, and when she saw the two weeping figures in the dark, the empty suit, the socks, the pocketbook, and the cuff links, she put down the tray on an armchair, looked piteously at the bent-over woman and the sobbing child and slipped away.

The idiot dropped himself down onto the floor. He pushed himself forwards with powerful movements of his hands towards the tray with the dainty morsels. He ate one after another indiscriminately.

Mrs. Littlemouse set to work sewing her undergarments that same night. She sewed dainty chemises for ladies, knickerbockers, petticoats, brassieres – she completed every piece conscientiously, with delicately embroidered hems, and finished off only half the quantity of undergarments which her cleverer colleagues managed.

She worked every day until twelve at night, and at five o'clock in the morning she started all over again. Nevertheless, the little girl got thinner and thinner. She got so thin that Mrs. Littlemouse interrupted her work one morning and took her to the hospital.

"She is malnourished," the Doctor said sternly, and Mrs. Littlemouse looked at him with a guilty expression.

"Well, she doesn't eat anything, Doctor. She always says she is fed up with potato soup. Do you understand?"

The doctor prescribed injections, which would stimulate the appetite, and in addition, to make her stronger, x-rays.[8] But then he saw her red hair and said that, if she was a redhead on top of everything, redheads could not withstand the treatment, and he sent the pair of them home. So Steffi was given an injection every other day, but she could still not eat the soup and that was all there was. Mrs. Littlemouse lost some of her customers but instead she now got sick pay for Steffi, who had to lie down all the time.

"I may not have any work any more, but instead I can nurse the child," she explained to Ljubka.

Ljubka had recently been very busy because the Prokops were preparing for a wedding. On the day of the wedding, the whole street was packed with cars. The wedding guests and especially Mrs. Prokops' numerous relatives all admired Tamara's spectacular wedding dress. The white bodice hugged her slim figure, she looked like a candle. The long train could of course be detached, for then the dress could be worn on the promenade at Biarritz.

Only the veil hung somewhat coarsely over her face, as Tamara had explained that you cannot use a veil for anything afterwards and had chosen the cheapest sort. And another thing puzzled the guests. How this delicate young creature was holding the roses in her hand! Tamara was not carrying the sweet-smelling roses as if they belonged to her. She was carrying them as if they were a burden rather than a symbol, something that she wanted to put away like an old umbrella, that's how. With the flowers pointed away from her, she stepped out of the Rolls Royce and onto the carpet which was spread out for her on the street, onto the carpet leading into the long corridor, and at the moment which Tamara entered followed by the guests, a coffin came towards her, a small coffin covered in black cloth. The guests made way. Mrs. Prokop went pale.

"That brings luck," she whispered thoughtfully into her sister's ear. A wrinkle appeared on Tamara's forehead. Knowing her mother as well as she did, that would cost her money. She looked in annoyance down at the ground and saw the roses in her hand. That gave her an idea; that way she would avoid expenses. Flowers faded anyway and you could not use them for anything. She passed them over to Mrs. Prokop and whispered something in her ear. Mrs. Prokop was afraid, however, and waved Ljubka over. Ljubka took the roses and weaved her way through the lines of guests and went up to the little coffin. She hesitated before she put the white roses on it. Mrs. Littlemouse did not see it. She was crying too much, she raised up her trembling arms, she wanted to tear the child out of the coffin. The two women, Mrs. Silk and the tenant, were holding her back. To begin with they had glanced hatefully at the wedding guests, but when they stepped politely aside and the fine gentlemen aired their bald patches, they made their peace too and arranged that the funeral bier did not take up too much room.

Tamara's husband looked admiringly at his beautiful young wife.

Notes

1. "Geduld bringt Rosen" by Veza Magd, first published in installments between 14-22 August 1932 in the *Arbeiter-Zeitung*. Reprinted in *Dreißig neue Erzähler des neuen Deutschland. Junge deutsche Prosa*, edited and with an introduction by Wieland Herzfelde (Berlin: Malik, 1932), pp. 93-126, and in *Geduld bringt Rosen* (1992), pp. 7-44.

2. The Prokops must have left Russia either directly after the Bolshevik Revolution in 1917 or during the 1920s in the aftermath of the Civil War.

3. Salubra, a German-based company founded in 1900, manufactured very fine wallpaper.

4. Elias Canetti makes similar use of the layout of Viennese townhouses in both *Auto-da-Fé* and his first play, *Wedding*, both written at about the same time as "Patience Brings Roses." His houses are both rather less complex than that inhabited by the Prokops and the Littlemouses, which has a "front house" giving on to the street, where the Prokops live on a higher story, and three courtyards, which would have been darker, less accessible, and therefore less desirable. In "Lost Property," Emma Adenberger's long address (3rd Courtyard, II Staircase, IV Floor, Flat 17a) gives an indication of the complexity of her building, which, in contrast, is likely to have contained only workers' apartments, like that in which Mrs. Shepherd is polishing the stairs in "Three Heroes and a Woman." Each house had a caretaker or concierge who was often known for officious enforcement of rules and for acting as a police spy.

Elias claimed to Ernst Fischer that the caretaker at 29 Ferdinandstraße would have denounced Fischer and his wife on 12 February 1934 had he seen them find refuge with the Canettis. He was the model for the brutal Benedikt Pfaff in his novel.

5. The Dorotheum, founded in 1707, has occupied a palais in the center of Vienna on the site of a former monastery since 1901, when it was opened by the Emperor Franz Josef. It remains to this day the most prestigious auction house in Central Europe.

6. Founded in 1876, an expensive hotel restaurant which became famous during the fin de siècle, not only for its fine food and lavish decor but also for its *chambres séparées*. In this context it is synonymous with decadence.

7. The Dianabad was first opened in 1808 and rebuilt in the splendid form Bobby and his friends would have known during the First World War.

8. X-rays could be prescribed at this time as therapy for various complaints. Canetti appears to have little faith in the practice since the doctor explains very unscientifically that they do not work on people with red hair. See also "Lost Property," where Dr. Spanek gives Emma Adenberger free x-ray treatment before propositioning her.

The Difference[1]

It was really impossible for people to go by without glancing happily at Käthi whenever she sat on the step in front of the house. She had tied a cord around her waist, and something hung from it at the side, but it was not a dagger. It was a little bag of marbles, and these gave her a feeling of enormous importance. The blue ones were her favorites, perhaps because they looked like her eyes. She moved the marbles around in the dirt, then wiped them on her knickers, put them back into the pouch where her dagger should have been, and looked like an angel who was being naughty. For in her pouch she had also hidden a sugar fish on a stick, and she licked at it from time to time, noting each time contentedly that the fish was still a long way from losing its shape.

The fish had naturally been a present, and it really was the least that Käthi would get as a present on any particular day. That's why she sat so happily on the steps in front of the house and laughed at the people who were so taken aback by her appearance. If two went by at once and they were women, they would stop, look at the child with the brown curls, look at her animated eyes, her doll's cheeks, then stare each other in the face and clap their hands together. "Well, I never!" they would call at the tops of their voices. "Well, I never! What a beautiful child!"

Perhaps it was the happy way that people looked at Käthi, which her own mother had so little time to do, that made her so cheerful; her mother was a servant. Käthi naturally knew nothing of this. She still had no idea that a mother always needs to perform a very low function in a different world as well as the high function she performed in her own world if she wants to have enough money to be a mother.

On her first day at school Käthi saw children sitting at the front in their new pinafores. She only had an old one made of a cheap kind of cloth, and her mother had sewn a big patch over the rip in the pocket, which stood out sharply on the faded material. And so she took her place at the back with the children who did not have new pinafores.

Käthi was immediately popular. The girls at the back with their yellow, thin faces were pleased that such a beautiful child was sitting next to them, and the model pupils at the front were not jealous of her because she was not a model pupil. Soon they developed a marvelous game of swap which they played under the desks and one day, when Käthi had already exchanged all her marbles as well as a silver clover leaf, a green crayon, a collapsing figure, and half a sheet of transfers, she brought in a bunch of red paper carnations. She had got them on 1 May when she was sitting at the front of the house and had looked with such delight at each passerby who was wearing one.[2] She had soon accumulated so many that Kurti Schleier, who was a year older and whose father was a banker, offered to sell them at a reduction of twenty percent and with fifty percent commission for his work. But she did not give up her carnations and did not decide until today that she would sacrifice them. Unfortunately, the teacher caught her just as she was swapping the carnations with her neighbor Hedi for a pencil case full of rubber shavings. The mistress's name was Schmidt, and because there were two mistresses with the same name in the school, the pupils called her "Big Schmidt." She came to the last row, looked disapprovingly at the red carnations, picked them up as if they were contaminated, and contemplated Hedi's rubber shavings with honest amazement, evidently reflecting on the unsolved mystery of what significance rubber shavings might have in the brain of a small girl.

It happened on this particular day that the mistress was taken ill and her colleague, "Little Schmidt," had to take her place. The girls sat as quietly as mice, which they had been ordered strictly to do; the ones in the back rows pressed their lips tightly together, but they suddenly found this very funny, and when Käthi saw how Franziska, one of the model pupils, was fighting off a fit of the giggles, she burst out giggling herself, which made all the others do the same. Thereupon, the mistress, Little Schmidt, stood in front of her and looked to see if she could identify the miscreants. All the faces immediately became serious. Only one could not hide her brightness, the redness of her cheeks, or the alertness of her eyes. "We will have to punish you," the mistress said in a way which was not unkind, and she bade Käthi stand behind the board. Käthi wanted to cry but thought to herself that there were no grounds for tears if she could be standing behind the board while the children at the front had to do sums. She also began to peep at the model pupils through a crack as they waited eagerly for the honor of being tested, and then she looked at her friends in the last two rows, who were fidgeting nervously because their turn would come soon. This made Käthi forget to watch out and consequently the mistress caught her again but remarkably sent her back to her place, trying not to smile.

Big Schmidt had meanwhile made a recovery and, stretching herself to her full height, she came into the classroom once more. From this height, the many little girls looked like flies - bothersome flies today, as she was in a bad mood.

"Come out," a voice said suddenly. Käthi did not even know that the voice meant her. "You shall go and say you're sorry!" Big Schmidt looked with unforgiving eyes at the red carnations which still lay reproachfully on the desk and looked with a similar reproach in her eyes at Käthi, her interrogating gaze resting on the patch on her pinafore.

"Please Miss, Franziska laughed too," Hedi called out and challenged Franziska with a stare, but she sat there in her sparkling pinafore and put on a virtuous expression. Big Schmidt did not even look at Hedi.

"You're coming with me," she said severely to Käthi and, turning to the class, "you will keep absolutely quiet!"

54 Veza Canetti

They walked down two long corridors and up three flights of stairs and went into Class B. Here all the girls were small like Käthi and she knew each one of them from the gym lesson. Big Schmidt's colleague was somewhat surprised when she arrived with the child.

"Say you're sorry immediately," said Big Schmidt and looked down at Käthi.

But Käthi could not say a word. Though her hair was sticking to her temples, her cheeks were burning and she did not move a muscle.

"You're the last person to put on airs. Just you wait until you go into service like your mother. Then you will learn how to be humble!"

At that point, all the little girls looked at Käthi as if she did not belong to them. Little Schmidt did not seem remotely delighted by the spectacle and gave Käthi a friendly prod in the direction of the door. She still had the same brave defiance in her face, but the curls around her temples did not dance any more. Her eyes looked quite dark. She crept slowly along the two long corridors and down the three flights of stairs – because for the first time in her life, she had learned that there was a difference.

Notes

1. "Die Grosse" by Martin Murner, first published 19 January 1933 in *Deutsche Freiheit*, reprinted 25 June 1933 in the *Arbeiter-Zeitung* under the name Martina Murner, and finally in *Der Fund* (Munich/Vienna: Hanser, 2001), pp.7-10. Martin Murner was the pseudonym of Carl von Ossietzky, journalist and editor of the satirical *Weltbühne*, who had been released from a year's jail sentence in December 1932 before being re-arrested after the Reichstag fire on 28 February 1933. He died in a concentration camp in 1938 after being injected with tuberculosis by his captors. He was awarded the Nobel Peace Prize in 1935.

2. Vienna witnessed mass processions each 1 May, international labor day, which were banned by Chancellor Dollfuß in 1933. Käthi thus gets into trouble at school for distributing flowers which were identified with the workers and the Social Democrats whose marches she has seen. 1 May is of great significance for Veza Canetti: she mentions it again in "The Criminal" as the name of the street where Georgie Burger and his father live; she published her last and arguably most political story, "Money - Money - Money," on 1 May 1937; and she died on 1 May 1963.

Then came four umbrellas, one after the other, then came a pair of gentleman's galoshes, then the assistant arrived with a briefcase containing a bathing suit, and then he arrived with a hedgehog. Knut would perhaps have been happy with the hedgehog, but despairing of finding anything original he took it for a hairbrush and paid it no attention. When the other employees saw his disappointment, they wanted to tease him, caught a mouse from behind the stove, and brought him the mouse. He was transported into such delight by the mouse that he suddenly got back his sunny expression; he laid it gently on his fingers and wished only that the person who had suffered the loss should not report it.

He looked for a long time for a suitable little place, found a parrot's cage, and lovingly shut the mouse in it. It would, for sure, have been impossible to tear him away from the cage had not more items of lost property arrived, a lady's goldwatch with chain, which Knut Tell did not even look at, and a lady's handbag. He opened the bag in a bad mood and was immediately taken with the six large keys which filled the inside of the bag. Then he gently pulled out an enormous handkerchief, which was carefully washed and ironed. Then he found a purse made of papier maché containing one schilling and a few groschen. Then he found a diary-notebook from two years ago, in which nothing was noted except the address of the owner, and the address sent Knut wild with excitement. It read:

Emma Adenberger
c/o Mrs. Kotrba
Am Katzensteg
Lamprechtsdorferstraße
3rd Courtyard, II Staircase, IV Floor, Flat 17a.

A piece of paper smeared with pencil would not have caught anyone else's attention, but for Knut Tell this piece of paper was reason enough to decide to stay on at his new job, and he went

Lost Property[1]

Knut Tell[2] had made the following return fro
poems: ten marks for a verse tribute, seventy-eight l
four dozen bookmarks, a cookery book, which he ha
competition, and a book plate, depicting a scepter, a ki
and a death's head as a crown. This is why his uncle
him: "Dear Nephew, you cannot carry on like this. This i
to live. I have a job for you at the Lost Property Office.
start tomorrow; you can write your poems in the evenin

This made Knut Tell's short nose terribly angry and h
of hair stand bolt upright so that he swept through the
room. "I am not going to do this!" he cried defiantly t
girlfriend Ruth. But Ruth was not born yesterday.

"Do you know, Knut? This is incredibly interesting.
imagine all the things that turn up there. Working out in y
mind whom each object belongs to, this is the right place fo
poet. Think of it as a way of getting ideas, Knut. Just go there f
a day, you lucky man, so that you can get an impression of all th
things that are brought in: each day they must get a globe, at th
very least, the most wonderful books - from the absent-minded
professors, don't you see? - chemical preparations which people
steal from the Panoptikum and then leave lying around because
they get scared.[3] That's what you will experience every day,
Knut!" (Once he's there, he will stay there, she thought to
herself.)

Knut Tell was keen. "That's the place to be, Ruth. The Devil
knows you're right."

Ruth made a face like an angel and straightaway telephoned
his uncle. The next morning Knut was standing punctually
behind the counter at the Lost Property Office.

The first item to be handed in was an old-fashioned bodice.

directly to the manager and reported that the name of the owner was in the bag and that he would return it to her after work. This made the manager telephone his uncle to say that his nephew was showing great diligence. On the piece of paper was written:

To Dr. Spanek

Once you said to me be Delicate towards women, but you have caused me pain. Coming to Teschen was my downfall.[4] In my Soul and in my Body and only because I Love you, never forgetting it. Nevertheless you did not see a Refined woman from the city in front of you but a Country girl, who you however shamed like she walked the streets. My cheeks go red from shame and tears come into my eyes when I think of it and when do I not do that. I wish to go Mad and not to have to think for once but that is not granted to me, you tell me yourself what Life can still be to me. I now say farewell and send best wishes, Your ...

Resi please write it up as soon as possible, correct the Mistakes dear child use the writing paper and if you send the packet as well then put all of it in a larger Envelope and ceale it up. My Sister is not to see it, she is so furious.

Knut Tell read the letter again and again. The mouse had meanwhile slipped out of the cage. The hedgehog had already eaten it, but Knut did not notice anything. He had thoughts the whole time only for the letter, and after work he ran to Katzensteg, through three courtyards, up to the fourth floor and he rang the bell of a battered door.

A young girl answered, so beautiful that Knut blushed.

"Excuse me," he said, "does this bag belong to you? It was handed in to us."

"Yes," said the girl and blushed too. "It's my bag. The keys in it are my landlady's. She would have made me replace them."

"The keys are there, only - the money is not quite right. It only had a little over a schilling in it."

"That's all there was. You can keep it for yourself. I haven't got any more. I'm out of a job."

"Oh," said Knut Tell regretfully, "have you lost your job?"

"No, I left of my own accord. It was a good job. Please, here is the money."

"I will take nothing. It's against the rules. I am from the Lost Property Office. I just want to ask, did you write this beauti... this letter, Miss?"

"That? Yes, I wrote it," she said and fell silent.

Knut Tell fell silent too. But there was nothing he would rather do than leave.

"I would just have liked to know, how ... how did you write this letter? Who is it to? But if you don't want to tell me, I can understand. It would just interest me terribly to know."

"It was my doctor in hospital. He gave me x-rays three times a week.[5] He was very good to me, even though I wasn't paying. He also asked me to go out with him on a Sunday. I didn't want to because the difference between us is too great. But when he was gone, I regretted it."

"Did he go away then?"

"He got himself a transfer. He didn't breathe a word of it to me and suddenly he was gone. Then I couldn't get any peace any more and I couldn't get work neither. Then I went back to the hospital and asked for his address. And then I left my job and - I followed after him."

"Did he write to you then?"

Emma lowered her head.

"Oh no, what you did is very beautiful. I am amazed by your courage. I admire you. It was very courageous, yes, really."

"I went straight to him from the train. And when a young lady answered, I had a terrible fright. She was very refined and when I said to her who I had come to see, she looked very unkindly at me. She led me into a large room and left me there. I couldn't have said a word on account of being so afraid. Then the door opened and he came in. She was behind him and he was quite horrified when he saw me and behaved as if I was a stranger. "You asked me out," I said, "and you once put it in writing and now you don't know me?"

"'I find it bizarre,' he said, 'that you have come here, young woman. Where is your sense of tact? You come here and infect the pure air of a lady. Do you not know what you owe to your station, and anyway, what do you want, Miss? Nothing whatsoever happened between us. I would like to make that clear. I demand that you make that clear to my fiancée. You come running after me and causing me trouble.'"

"Please don't cry," Knut consoled her. "He's a quite horrific person. Please, don't cry. You are ..."

"Doctor, that is not why I have come, I say," Emma Adenberger continued. "Nothing happened between us. I can make that clear, all right."

"Oh please, don't cry. The fellow does not deserve it. I will show him. I will hit him in the face!" Knut was on the point of setting off directly for Teschen.

"No, please, don't do anything to him. He was always good to me and was always polite in the hospital, even though I didn't pay. He was just afraid of her. She had such unkind eyes. If he could only see how unkind she is. He will marry her and be unhappy."

"Don't cry."

"I ran off straight away because I couldn't stand her eyes."

"And why did you write him this ... this letter?"

"I didn't want it all to end in such an ugly way. That's why I also sent him the gold watchchain, so he doesn't have to be ashamed of me."

"I thank you," said Knut Tell and shyly took her hand. He shook it energetically, wanted to say something else, saw the beautiful girl stand there embarrassed, and ran away like a thief, for he had hidden the piece of paper in his fist.

At home he wrote a long story all through the night about

the girl and he fell so in love with his character that he also began a letter to her and asked her to marry him. It was already morning when his head lolled to one side and he fell asleep on the couch.

Ruth came at midday and found him breathing heavily, his cheeks hot. His papers were spread out across the table. Ruth began to read the story and smiled delightedly. But then she also read the letter and slapped Knut in the face. That made Knut dream that a glacier had fallen on his head and he awoke with a start. When he saw Ruth's angelic face, he smiled, but Ruth cursed like a devil. "You're going to get married, are you, going to get married?"

"Ruth," said Knut, genuinely baffled, "do you want to marry me then?"

"As if the thought would cross my mind," she cursed. "You and getting married. You will never marry anybody, understand?"

"But I'm not thinking of doing any such thing, Ruth. What gives you such an idea?" he asked innocently.

Then Ruth realized that he had just been building castles in the air again, but his keenness ...

"And what's happening with the Lost Property Office, Knut?"

"But you said yourself, I should just go for a day," said Knut, who stretched himself out and carried on sleeping.

Notes

1. "Der Fund" by Martina Murner, first published 28 April 1933 in the *Arbeiter-Zeitung*, reprinted in *Der Fund* (2001), pp.11-17.

2. Knut Tell appears too in the first chapter of *Yellow Street* ("The Monster") and in *The Tiger*. He is thought to be a satirical portrait of Veza's husband-to-be, the unpublished novelist, Elias Canetti, who describes his practice of hunting down linguistic material he can make use of in his writing in volume two of his autobiography, *The Torch in the*

Ear. Ruth is an authorial alter ego but shares her name with Ernst Fischer's new wife, Ruth von Mayenburg, one of Elias's many female admirers.

3. The Panoptikum was an attraction at the Prater Funfair which showed tableaux of famous historical scenes, similar to Madame Tussauds in London. In *The Tongue Set Free* Elias describes his terror as a young child standing in front of the Earthquake at Messina. Herr Vlk in *Yellow Street* likes gazing at the scenes of execution.

4. Dr. Spanek would appear to have had enough of Vienna: Silesian Teschen, which had been ruled by the Habsburgs since the Middle Ages, was the military headquarters for the Austro-Hungarian forces during the First World War. It was divided between Poland and Czechoslovakia after 1918 and taken by Poland after the Munich Conference in September 1938.

5. See "Patience brings Roses," note 8.

The Poet[1]

The earliest memory that we have is that the covering over
us is made of green leaves, which seem as if they are lying on top
of our eyes because we are pushed in prams through parks and
down avenues. But Gustl's first impressions were vertical. He
was carried around by his mother on her arm, carted about, one
could almost say, like a sheaf of corn, and he saw colors, posts,
bright lights, and took such fright that his face was soon no more
expressive than a baby monkey's.

When he could walk, he played on the dirt road in front of
the yard. When the sun was high in the sky, a large woman would
come to the meadow with two children, turn her back on him,
and sit down on the bench. The children would turn around
curiously to see him. One day he was eating the bread which had
been prepared for his lunch. He liked smelling it, the air was
delicious, the sun did not stint on its warmth. Both children
envied him as he sat the way he wanted on the road and played
in the dirt.

"That's how you catch diseases from your food," the
governess explained and pointed at Gustl's dirty hands. They got
cleaner with every mouthful of bread which slipped down into
his stomach, along with the dirt. He enjoyed eating the bread but
then he wished that he had not done so. From that point
onwards, he often yearned to be growing up like the boy and girl
on the bench in the meadow. He often felt quite unhealthy, and
nowadays he rubbed his fingers vigorously before he took a
mouthful of bread.

At school the teacher was used to assaulting the children
with questions. This always made Gustl so scared that he could
not utter a word. When they were practising Roman numerals, he
was horrified when he saw the thick stems that he was drawing

as shadows for his strokes. He looked admiringly at the fine strokes drawn by the boy next to him. They looked clean while his own were dirty. When the teacher moved down the rows, he stopped in front of Gustl to look at his book. And it was his numerals rather than anyone else's which the teacher found the most beautiful. On this day Gustl made a notch in his long stick which he kept hidden in his chest. He did that whenever he had a special experience.

If it was raining, he had to stay in his room. The window looked out on to a long row of backyards. Directly in front of his window was a roof. Sometimes a tiny mouse ran around on it. Apart from that, everything was dead. Once on a dreary day, he could not think of anything to amuse himself. So he stood at the window and looked at the empty roof. It was so sad looking at the roof, especially because he knew nothing about himself. For this reason he tried not to be distracted and instead just stared at the emptiness. He never forgot this day.

On a day when it was raining, he kept himself busy by scraping the window sill with a knife. Underneath the brown paint you could see the beautiful wood. Then he gave himself a little cut on his finger. And then he saw a rubber band emerge from the scraped-off wood, the sort one used to wrap around little parcels. He ran to his mother, who grabbed the knife from his hand but said nothing about the miracle of the rubber band.

On fine days the two children came on time to the bench. The boy refused to be forbidden from speaking to Gustl.

"My name is Jobst. My father is a landowner, and yours?"

"I don't have one," said Gustl and looked up at him, overwhelmed by the boy's brutal health and glacial eyes. Jobst took possession of his toy. It hurt Gustl to watch him do so, but he admired him for it. One day Jobst had a real locomotive on rails. The boy looked at it, touched it, and picked it up with that disdain which rich children have for their toys. Gustl looked on with fear and shyness at how the machine was wound up, how it ran, how it stopped, how the boy moved it forward with his foot, how he wound it up again, turning the key too far and breaking it. Then he put the dead thing down and hurried to his governess. Gustl went home trembling. He hated the boy.

One time the little girl came to the bench on her own with the governess. Gustl brought out his new ball which he used to keep hidden from Jobst.

The ball bounced very high and landed near the bench. The little girl pushed it back with her foot. Then she stole a glance at her governess, who wore glasses and was reading the newspaper, then hopped up quietly and took up position to play ball with Gustl. Neither spoke a word. They just smiled happily because the spell had been broken.

"Nelli!" a voice screeched out, "you're not allowed to play with that boy!"

The girl dropped the ball obediently and sat back down on the bench in embarrassment. Gustl went home. He fretted for a long time over why the little girl was not allowed to play with him. It made him feel very ashamed.

When he could read by himself, it seemed to him as if he had been born for a second time. Everything before was dull. But a book is quickly read and now began his hunger for new books. For one whole afternoon he picked up the balls for the landowner's son as he was playing tennis. Jobst promised him *Gulliver's Travels* in return. When they had finished, Gustl stood before him, his heart beating wildly. Jobst bounced over to his governess. "He wants to borrow my Gulliver."

"You aren't allowed to lend any of your books."

"I'm not allowed to lend any of my books," Jobst called back excitedly. It was plain by looking at him how glad this made him.

Gustl went home and carved a diagonal notch in his wooden stick. He became so shy that he never told a story himself but always just listened. The schoolboys all dumped their dissatisfaction at his door. They brought all of it to him. They all thought they were better than him but still liked him.

"I'm going to be a pilot," said the classmate to his right.

"I'm going to be a mayor," said the other to his left.

"And me a diplomat."

"And me a captain of a frigate."

Only Gustl did not know what he wanted to be. His mother did not know either. In summer she worked outside in the fields; in winter she knitted on her machine. He felt terribly sorry for her.

When the first free compositions came to be written, the teacher saw that not everything that Gustl had heard during all his years at school had passed him by without making an impression. Indeed, he even gained a reputation for his essays. The teacher in the highest class got him a job as house tutor to an English family. His employers took him with them to the capital and allowed him to continue with his own studies. At a tender age he was rewarded with a position in a state school and won over the boys with his fanatical enthusiasm for the practice of justice. His superiors pressed him to write down his method. But when he set to work, turbulent descriptions came out instead of drily technical impressions, and it turned out that he had the stuff of a poet in him. He was immediately asked to write down his life story.

To do this he went back to his little home town. A thick wall fenced off the estate of Junker Jobst, who could not be wished away from his childhood memories. But the servants did not know the Junker. The estate did not belong to him any more. He had frittered away his money and in the end had resorted to cheating at cards. He asked after the young mistress. The fragile young girl had married a tavern keeper's son and been rejected by her family on that account. He went into the inn which in his day had been frequented by his classmates. There they all sat together at the regulars' table. The diplomat was an undertaker, the captain an assistant manager in the post office, the pilot a barber. Only the mayor had really become a mayor. He was the richest man in the place. He was cursing that he always caught a cold in winter at funerals because he had to take his hat off when the coffin was lowered into the ground. Then they all fell silent for a while. None of them could think of anything appropriate to say. Nobody recognized the classmate of days gone by in the young man at the next table. The inn regulars did not penetrate his deep seriousness.

A waitress brought him beer and cheese.

"Nelli!" the undertaker called over from the regulars' table. "A glass of wine."

Gustl looked at her in fright. The woman he saw before him had long ago forgotten that she had once sat next to the governess and was not allowed to play with him. He continued listening to the regulars' tedious conversation for a while. They were all old and desiccated before their time. He paid, hiding his face as he did so. At home his mother had arranged everything festively.

In the trunk over in the corner was the wooden stick with the straight and diagonal notches. They were the chapters in the novel of his life.

In her best dress his mother served up the food. Her chapped hands were now able to rest.

Notes

1. "Der Dichter" by Martina Murner, first published 3 August 1933 in the *Arbeiter-Zeitung*, reprinted 12 July 1934 in *Deutsche Freiheit* and in *Der Fund* (2001), pp.18-22.

The Criminal[1]

On the "Street of the 1st of May" George Burger the wild-animal breeder is standing in front of the exotic display in his shop window, pulling snakes which are poisonous, but only to other animals, from out of his box – giant snakes, but with brightly colored patterns, and modern snakes, fat and greedy, but useful for ladies' handbags.[2]

"This crocodile is tiny but the crocodile inside is three metres long and one-hundred-and-twenty years old and extremely dangerous! Take a look at the ape breastfeeding her young. Here you see the purity of the mother ape's love for her child. Step inside, ladies and gentlemen. Fifty groschen a ticket, children half price."

Little Georgie is standing next to his father the wild-animal breeder and looking up at him in admiration. He holds the snakes in his hand, folded in two like pieces of string; young lads stare with open mouths. Georgie is so keen that he doesn't even see how the onlookers slink away and walk on and how anxiously his father looks after them. Times are bad. Georgie hasn't the remotest idea that this is so, and how should he if the wild-animal breeder George Burger does not let his boy notice that he is poor, as we will now see him do?

"George," said Georgie dreamily (he called his father by his first name), "will you let me go on the Big Dipper today?"

"The Big Dipper, lad? Didn't I read you the story in the newspaper? Oh no, I read it with your mother, about the Big Dipper coming off the rails yesterday? Twenty people fell to the ground. You mustn't even go near it or one of the people will fall on you!"

"And the Haunted Castle?"

"The Haunted Castle? They have ghosts in there and wicked

devils and death's heads and dragons and knifemen! They're all made out of wood, of course, but you get a terrible fright. Today they carried out an old lady because she fainted."

"And what will happen to me if I go in the electric car, George?" Georgie was enjoying it already.

"In the electric car! Can you remember the automatic machine? Well, that was just a small shock. The car will give you a shock which goes through your whole body."

"And the shooting range, George?"

"Last week a plank of wood sprang back and hit a boy right on the nose. Now he's running about the place with his nose swollen."

"And the Big Wheel?" Georgie looked in wonder into his father's kind eyes.

"One in three boys has to climb on to the roof while it's going round. That's what they make you do. Just don't go on it, but now you have to be off, my lad. Work is starting. – Ladies and gentlemen! Inside we will show the only flying dog in Europe!"

Flying Dog is the name of the Indian Chief, thought Georgie and off he flew. He stopped in front of the Haunted Castle. Four fat women were deciding whether or not to go in.

"Whatever you do, don't go in there," said Georgie, "an old woman had a stroke in there today. She dropped down dead."

The women ran away in fright.

His hands in his pockets Georgie strolled sweetly through the crowd and went up to the Big Dipper. The whole of Class A from the secondary school was there waiting to go on it. Class B was in detention.

"I wouldn't go on that if I were you," said Georgie mysteriously, "a hundred crashed yesterday. They were all bloody and some of them fell on me!"

The prefect who was buying the tickets was astonished to see the boys suddenly run off, after they had pestered him to let them go on the Big Dipper.

"What shall we go on, Georgie?" asked Peterheinz.

Georgie looked at him earnestly. "Well, try the Tunnel of Fun," he suggested, as George had not said anything about that.

And so the old dust-covered Tunnel of Fun was honored by a visit and the old dust-covered owner who was taking the money woke up. Georgie wandered in with the other boys, and soon the prefect who was counting noticed there was one boy too many, but Georgie slipped in with the rest of them.

"Are you by any chance Georgie Hacker who wrote the Diary of a Naughty Boy?" Peterheinz asked him.

"My name isn't even Hacker, but Burger, like George, who has a really beautiful animal show. There is a crocodile as big as the whole Tunnel of Fun. You can't put your hand out. It would eat every one of you up. Every day it eats a whole rabbit.'

The wild-animal breeder George Burger was taken aback when his little son turned up with a long queue of boys who paid him good money, with just a small reduction because there were so many of them. After the animal show they smuggled Georgie into the movie theater.

The film was called *Emil and the Detectives*, but it had started a long while ago, so they saw the middle first. Suddenly there was a noise from among the audience.[3] A finely dressed woman was confronting a man who looked around helplessly and was not wearing a collar. Georgie liked him immediately, as George always said that having no collar was no disgrace. Being rich was the only thing which was disgraceful. The program seller went up to the man and asked him to leave.

"I only came in half an hour ago," the man kept on saying. You could see by looking at him that he had gone without a meal to buy the movie ticket.

"It says five o'clock on your ticket. You have to go."

"But he came in with us," Georgie called out in excitement. He squeaked a little as he spoke, for he really was still a very small boy.

The employee paid him no attention. The man did not stir

from his seat. The well-dressed woman was waiting with hostile intent. Then the manager, who had been sitting taking the money, appeared.

"Just see that you get out," he roared at the man without a collar and it hurt Georgie's heart to see him look around and for nobody to take his side.

"Excuse me, he can have my ticket," Georgie now called out, as loudly as he could from out of his slender body. The boys looked at him admiringly. But then he had a fright. He didn't even have a ticket himself. He had been smuggled in by the boys. His cheeks burned red.

"The tickets are not transferrable," the program seller said, to Georgie's relief, and the manager shook the poor man by the shoulder and pushed him out. The audience hissed their approval.

"But he did come in with us," said Georgie to the boys, looking threateningly at the manager. "I'm not staying a moment longer, lads. George always says you don't have to start looking among the common folk if you're looking for criminals."

The audience laughed, but Georgie didn't care about all the people. He shook Peterheinz and the other boys by the hand and strode out of the theater as if he were wearing seven-league boots.

Notes

1. "Der Verbrecher" by Veza Magd, first published 31 August 1933 in the *Arbeiter-Zeitung*, reprinted 7 September 1933 in *Deutsche Freiheit* and in *Geduld bringt Rosen* (1992), pp.57-63.

2. George and Georgie Burger work on the edge of the Prater, two of the main attractions of which were the Big Wheel and the Grottenbahn (or "Tunnel of Fun"), which Elias describes in some detail in *The Tongue Set Free*: "There were lots of things in the Tunnel of Fun, but only one thing counted. I certainly looked at the gaudy groups that came first, but

I only pretended: Snow White, Red Riding Hood, and Puss in Boots; all fairy tales were nicer to read, in tableaux, they left me cold. ... the train halted briefly in front of each one, and I was so annoyed at the superfluous wait that I cracked silly jokes about the fairy tales, spoiling my brothers' fun. They, in contrast, were utterly unmoved when the chief attraction came: the Earthquake at Messina." Elias Canetti, *The Tongue Set Free. Remembrance of a European Childhood,* translated by Joachim Neugroschl, in *The Memoirs of Elias Canetti* (New York: Farrar, Straus, and Giroux, 1999), pp.86-87.

3. Erich Kästner's 1928 novel was filmed by Gerhard Lamprecht in 1931 and starred Fritz Rasp as the thief.

New Boy[1]

Seidler had such good references from his years of loyal service working as a cashier that he got a job as a supervisor in a factory. He did checks in the department where the yarn was wound into spools and then boxed into rows, and when work finished, he had to search every worker for spools of yarn. Whenever he felt down the pockets of his fellow human beings and hit against a hidden spool, he failed to bat an eyelid and let them through. The workers liked him, but that was precisely what cost him the bosses' favor, and he lost his job.

His good references and especially the reference supplied by his honest face stood him in good stead a second time. He was given a job as a sales assistant in an elegant jeweler's shop, and now it was his own pockets which were searched when he left the shop each evening. There were, however, other strange practices at Kranz & Son, Jewelers. His fingerprints, for example, were photographed, and he was only allowed to touch the boxes in the shop window if he put on woolen gloves, so that in case of a robbery they could identify the thief's fingerprints. It was not long before his managers realized that they did not have to search his pockets, but they also realized that his good character and willingness to please were not enough. Seidler did not know how to talk a customer into buying any jewelry because he did not understand what the jewelry was worth. The whole business seemed ridiculous to him – the ladies who spent hours bent over fragments of crystal, magnifying-glass in hand, the bosses who bowed and scraped to the ladies, forgetting the dignity which they maintained at other times, and he thought his own behavior was ridiculous too, pretending that all this was important. A day which began with him forgetting to put on his gloves when he arranged the shop window, which luckily nobody noticed, finished with him allowing a customer to get away, which everyone noticed, and then he had to go himself.

Now he was sitting next to those who had lost their hope and was waiting for work. A friend who still owed him a favor from his time at the factory told him about a newspaper which was just being set up. He went straight to the editor's office, showed his references, and got the best job in our city, in front of our most beautiful church.[2] There were already four people representing other newspapers of various political persuasions. The man with a bowtie under his chin and dressed in a brown suit sold the German newspapers. In addition there was a man from the *Austrian*, another from the *Extra*, and a woman selling the *Telegraph*. If she needed change, she shouted "Hitler!" and the man dressed in brown gave her change. If he didn't have any, she called "Extra!" and the man from the *Extra* helped her out. There was no political wrangling between them. There was just the hunt for customers, the hunt for bread, and their hatred was reserved for the rain, which was bad for business, or for beggars who distracted the customers, and most of all they hated a newcomer, who could mean competition. Seidler was this newcomer. The four whispered to each other whenever he came near, and the man dressed in brown turned up with a pipe the following day and stuffed it full of wool to blow the smoke into the newcomer's face, so that his voice croaked and he could not shout, a superfluous precaution. New newspapers don't sell by themselves. You have to stick at it until you have made a breakthrough.

The newcomer did stick at it and shouted out the name of his newspaper hoarsely and much too bashfully. This made him look small and submissive, like a little gothic statue. Once he tried to help the woman from the *Telegraph* when she wanted to change a fifty groschen coin, but she would rather let the customer walk on than accept his money and, not knowing what else to do, his hand sank back down to his side. He cut such a sorry figure next to the self-confident gestures of the man in brown, who held out his paw-like hand full of German newspapers and yelled his "Heil!" to every customer, that the passersby noticed Seidler and bought his paper. Their new habit grew, which was why he was able to bring in a small profit earlier than anticipated.

But one day two men appeared in front of him. They showed him they were detectives, called him over, and told him directly that he was arrested on suspicion of theft. There had been a break-in at Kranz & Son, Jewelers, and his fingerprints were the only ones which had been found. When a human being has to struggle all his life against the temptation of ending his misery by putting his hand in the till, which would not significantly have harmed anybody, by removing a piece of jewelery, whose removal would hardly have been noticed, when a human being defies all these temptations, he can feel himself brought so low by a false accusation that he blushes and stutters. Tears come to his eyes. He does not know what to say and behaves just as if he were guilty. And that is what Seidler did. He asserted his innocence later to the examining magistrate, but he got sent to prison anyway because they had made enquiries among the tell-tales, and the man in brown had said that he had immediately seemed suspicious to him, scared-looking, with his guilty conscience written all over his face.

Seidler sat in his cell, looking as if he was being whipped by invisible tormentors, but nobody understood his despair. Then the door opened and a man entered whom he didn't think he had seen before. It was not until he opened his mouth that he recognized his friend from the factory. "What are you doing in jail," said the friend, "when I can remember very well that you once arranged the shopwindow without putting on your gloves. Instead of speaking out you let yourself be locked up! I have made a statement. This is not the place for you." Seidler was released less than an hour later, as they could not find a scrap of evidence against him. He also got back his old place in front of the church, but the atmosphere there had not improved. What's more his nerves were in tatters after the fright of the last few days, and he did not possess nearly enough strength to get himself back on his own feet. Wearily he shouted out the name of his paper, his eyes screwed up in the corners of their sockets, as if he were fighting back the tears. Suddenly he had a fright. The two detectives were standing there again, and there he stood, defenseless and expecting more hard and unjust treatment. But what was happening? They walked past. They went up to the man with the German papers, they took him to one side, they took him away from the stand with his papers, and they led him away. The three all began talking excitedly to one another and looked maliciously at the newcomer as if he were the cause of these events, and the detectives came back directly, this time without the man in brown.

They went up to the tell-tales and it turned out that passersby had repeatedly complained about how loud and aggressively the man in brown used to shout. And it turned out further that a house search had uncovered quantities of explosives in his possession and that the police had been looking for him for a long time. The tell-tales were now questioned by the police, but they did not give him away. The two detectives now approached Seidler and looked at him in a friendlier way than usual. Now Seidler would have had enough to say about his colleague's tirades, but he just explained that he stood off to the side from the others and didn't know anything about it. "Your colleague did not behave so well towards you, though," said one of the officers sharply but tipped his hat politely nonetheless and went off with the other one.

"That was good of him," the *Austrian* said loudly, so that the newcomer could hear, and the *Extra* went to stand right next to him. The woman from the *Telegraph* waited impatiently for the next customer and called out a little shyly: "Hey, Pinko! Get change!"

Notes

1. "Der Neue" by Veza Magd, first published 23 November 1933 in the *Arbeiter-Zeitung*, reprinted in *Geduld bringt Rosen* (1992), pp.65-72.

2. This is the Stephansdom, Vienna's medieval cathedral which stands at the center of the city within view of the Leopoldstadt where Canetti lived.

Three Heroes and a Woman[1]

Mrs. Shepherd was standing on the landing and washing the stairwell. Even though all the steps shimmered with polish, she kept on rubbing over them with the wet cloth, pushing noisily into the corners with the broomstick, then shoving the cloth into the bucket before wringing it out and wrapping it once more round the broom. The cloth made a splashing noise when it hit the steps, and had anyone been watching Mrs. Shepherd's actions and the expression on her face they would have understood: her mind was not on the task at hand. She was preoccupied by an image. No matter how hard she reasoned with herself, she could not get this image out of her head. It was a small church which she saw in front of her, a small church that tormented Mrs. Shepherd. The church had the strange reputation of making every wish that was uttered in it come true.

Mrs. Shepherd was not a believer, but when her husband was in the war and she received the news that he had been badly wounded, she dragged herself into the church and sank to her knees. Her husband came back from the war and ever since then a tender smile passed Mrs. Shepherd's lips every time someone uttered the name of the church.

Until the dreadful thing happened.

It began when the workers who lived in the municipal apartment houses were fired on with cannons by their brothers.[2] The big municipal apartment house where Mrs. Shepherd had worked for years had to surrender, the weapons were given up, and the workers fled through an underground passage into the little church. They thought they were safe. One after another, drunk with joy, they staggered out of the church to freedom and *each* one who stepped out of the church was shot down on the spot...

Suddenly Mrs. Shepherd awoke with a jolt. Still startled, she turned her head. After yanking wildly at the glass door a gang of young men stormed through it and up the steps towards her. Strange, they all had the same expression on their faces. With the fear of death in their eyes, they beseeched her with looks. Then one of them, embarrassed, raised his hand to implore her, but listlessly let it drop down again.

She immediately understood and all manner of thoughts raced through her head. She thought the boys looked just like her son Franz when they had hidden him from the cannons in the cellar, where he was safer than in the accursed miracle church. She thought they wanted to be rescued, like him, and were young, like Franz too, and each one of them had a mother too. Then she thought what lay in store for her if she helped the boys and her chin quivered.

But she said, "Second floor, door number five," and let them through.

The boys stormed up the stairs, blind with fear, to door number five. If there were going to be difficulties there, it was too late now. At number five, the door opened silently by itself, not a priest but a worker stood behind it, and without making a sound he gestured for them to pass, and the lads became as quiet as mice. As quietly as mice they followed the directions of the widely outstretched arms that had let them in, with warm, happy, grateful looks on faces which had moments before looked frightened to death. And the protective door closed behind them.

Down below Mrs. Shepherd heard the lock snap shut and at just that moment the glass door was pushed open. Two policemen all but skewered Mrs. Shepherd on their bayonets. An officer came after them.

"This is where the fellows ran in," he shouted.

"I beg your pardon?" said Mrs. Shepherd and leaned on her broom handle.

"This is where the red dogs ran in. Don't mess around with me, or there'll be trouble!"

"Chief Inspector! The house has sixteen stair-wells. Noone has come through! I would have seen them, I have been washing here for more than an hour!"

"They won't get away from us," said the Chief Inspector and banged on the door of number one. "Who lives here?"

Mrs. Shepherd looked fearfully down at the floor and was even more scared by what she saw. On the damp steps there shimmered about twenty sets of footprints, smudged into one another, forming large, menacing stains on the steps, which just three minutes ago had shimmered with polish.

The Chief Inspector had no time to look down from his great height. He was busy hitting the door of number one. "Oh, please, don't knock at this one! Mrs. Green the seamstress lives here. She has been in a fright for days now. She gets a screaming fit at the slightest thing. She lives all by herself. She can't have let anyone in. I was standing here. I would have seen it for sure. Take a look in all the apartments, Chief Inspector, but not Mrs. Green's!"

The Chief Inspector looked at her slyly and tore so hard at the bell that the knob came off in his hand. He threw it contemptuously onto the floor. A woman as thin as a piece of thread opened the door a crack and was pushed aside by the Chief Inspector. The second policeman remained standing at the door.

Mrs. Shepherd picked up her broom. Only her ears still had their human functions, for while her arms swept over the steps like pistons and wiped away the clues in frantic haste, her ears were the eyes in the back of her head. She was just dipping the cloth into the bucket again when the Chief Inspector came out. Inside the seamstress was having a screaming fit.

"Who lives here!" said the Chief Inspector irritably and kicked at the door of number two.

"The furrier Cibulka lives here. No sign that he let anyone in, Chief Inspector. He's very particular with his furs. A single one costs a hundred schillings, he always says. I wouldn't bother yourself with him. They hang down from all over his ceiling. Something will fall on your head."

The Chief Inspector knocked so hard the furrier Cibulka came out of his flat. Without waiting for an invitation, they entered his workshops, while the second policeman waited at the door with raised firearm.

"Leave that alone!" Mrs. Shepherd heard Cibulka say inside. She was moving the broom more calmly now over the steps. They had almost got their old shimmer back. "Your honor, a few fellows have run away from you into the house. Should they have given themselves up to your cannons?"

"Shut your mouth! Stupid Czech!" screamed the Chief Inspector.

"In Prague, where I come from they don't fire on their own people!"

After saying this, Mr. Cibulka was ordered to come with them, but he put up resistance. "I'm not scared," he shouted.

The Chief Inspector had the choice of exchanging a large prey for a small one, and contented himself with taking down Mr. Cibulka's details. Mrs. Shepherd had suddenly become quiet. The Chief Inspector stomped up to the second floor, his companions in tow.

"Chief Inspector, please knock quietly here. The shoemaker Pfeidl lives here. His wife is dying in bed. They shot her son yesterday as he ran out of the church. She hasn't got long to go."

"Open up!" screamed the Chief Inspector, and the shoemaker Pfeidl put up no resistance. The Chief Inspector saw the dying woman who was holding a man's blood-stained coat in her knotted fingers. Rather put out, he stepped outside.

"You'd better knock at five, but not four," said Mrs. Shepherd without being asked. "At four they're all dead, the husband and two sons. The wife hanged herself yesterday. Only the grandmother is inside. She has gone mad with grief. She won't open the door. Her niece is not coming until midday."

The Chief Inspector knew straightaway that the bandits were

hidden at number four; the two policemen broke the door down. In the bare room an old woman sat at the window and looked at the intruders with eyes which were dead. The Chief Inspector was still obsessed with this flat and searched each room. He even glanced over his shoulder as he left to see if ten men had not after all hidden themselves there.

"Who lives here?" he asked in a rather subdued tone on stepping outside and pointed at number five.

The cleaning woman looked death in the eye. The danger was so great that she became quite calm.

"This is where the servant woman Neumann lives. She is at work the whole day, but the child is at home, little Steffi. I can call her and she will come straightaway if she hears me."

"Bah!" said the Chief Inspector, who was not impressed by the prospect of scaring a child. "Leave it. Let's go!" he commanded and went back down with his companions without looking back in Mrs. Shepherd's direction.

And that was good. For no sooner had the glass door closed, than Mrs. Shepherd sank down on to the steps.

The lads spent the night in quiet conversation and the worker who lived at number five woke up at the same time as they and fetched his sister-in-law, the cleaning woman, into the flat.

In the morning the first dove was sent out with a milkcan. Lots of workers go through the enormous municipal house in the mornings and the first one got through unscathed. The second carried a briefcase. An hour later they were all in freedom.

Notes

1. "Drei Helden und eine Frau" by Veronika Knecht, first published
July 1934 in *Neue deutsche Blätter. Monatsschrift für Literatur und Kritik*,
reprinted in *Geduld bringt Rosen* (1992), pp.73-82.

2. On 12 February 1934, in response to a workers' revolt orchestrated
by elements of the defunct Republican Defense League, Chancellor
Dollfuß used artillery against the Goethehof and the Karl-Marx-Hof,
two of the Social Democrats' proudest post-1918 housing develop-
ments. The events in the story are fictional but could be based in part
on Canetti's own role in sheltering Ernst and Ruth Fischer for the night
of 12 February while her mother, who died in October that year, lay
seriously ill.

Clairvoyants[1]

I felt my hair standing on end. I found myself in Minna's room. It was four o'clock in the afternoon. The clock on the wall showed the time and I could hear it ticking. There was no other sound. I recognized everything - the modern furniture in Minna's room and the old-fashioned photographs on the wall, the learned books on the shelf and the homely proverb in a picture frame, the glass-topped modernist table with a vase of artificial flowers on it. Everything was as it should be. Except what was that on the little coffee table? How could that be? Was she mad? I reassured myself that she must have got them from the Anatomical Institute. Chopped-off hands, tautly elongated, as stiff as death!

I was so dazed by the grisly sight of these chopped-off hands displayed in front of me, still pink with blood at the roots, right here in Minna's room, that I had quite a start when the door opened. Minna came in.

"Welcome," she said. "Aren't they brilliantly done? They were made by an Englishman. He works for Madame Tussauds. But that is not the point which is interesting. What is interesting is the owner of these hands. He's a mesmerist. We have just been talking about how wonderful it is that the divine power should reside not only in the brain and eyes, but also in the hands." Minna's own kind, fanatical eyes flickered anxiously. Without saying a word she pulled me into the next room. The other guests were either standing or sitting, mute and motionless. I hope they're not made of wax as well, I thought with a fright. I went up to the first lady in the row. "She's the pianist," Minna whispered. The pianist had a great big nose and small, weak eyes. I then introduced myself to a patron of the arts, a waiter, a circus rider, and a lady who was hard of hearing. "Introduced myself" is the right way to put it. The initiative was all mine. They looked at me icily. At last with the glacier behind me, I stood in front of Antonia. Antonia is very pretty but only when she is sitting down. When she is standing up, she measures six feet two.

"Why is Minna so excited?" I whispered to her and sat down next to her on the sofa.

"Because the clairvoyant is coming."

"Is he exciting?"

"Terribly!"

"Are you excited too?"

"Indescribably!"

"Can he tell fortunes?"

"He can see into the future!" Antonia corrected me.

"Whose future has he foretold?" I asked and pointed to the assembled company.

"Everyone's."

"What did he say to her?" I pointed to the circus stuntwoman.

"She gets shot at every evening as she rides round the track - with arrows. She couldn't go on doing it any more because she was so scared. He calmed her down. Now she won't have an accident."

"And what did he say to him ...?" I pointed to the waiter.

"He used to run a hotel and can speak eight languages. He will inherit some money and buy another hotel. And the gentleman over there is a well-known patron of the arts. He has fallen on hard times and lives from selling his pictures. In his case, the clairvoyant saw immediately that he has a serious lung disease. But no one must tell him. It was fortunate that he controlled himself on that occasion. Sometimes he cannot control himself at all and lets out the most terrible truths."

"Who's he going to do today?"

"You!"

"*Me?*"I tried to smile in a superior sort of way but inside I had a fright. I despised myself for it. But suddenly there I was, sitting peacefully with the rest of them, sitting and waiting. With noone saying a word.

A tall, slim gentleman entered the room, with eyes which made him look as if he were blind. Everyone got up. As Antonia, who was next to me, stood up, I had to stand up too. "Who's that then?" I asked.

"That's him." Antonia's eyes glinted with enthusiasm. But because she was so big, it looked as if she were going to swallow the thin gentleman whole. He himself greeted them all with condescension and me with contempt.

Then he sat down at a round table and the guests did the same. Minna pulled me on to a chair next to her.

They had better ask me if I agree to all this, I thought to myself. I would rather not let myself be "seen through." You just get scared for nothing and feel embarrassed. I wanted to spell this out to Minna, but the words got stuck in my mouth. All eyes in the room were fixed on me. The clairvoyant had got up. His pallor was deathly. There were drops of cold sweat on his forehead. He stretched out a thin, white hand and pointed at me with his finger.

"You have something in your head," he blurted out. "In your head. It's painful. A tumor," he said.

I reached for my head, choking with fear. I did indeed suffer from headaches and lately they had been especially bad. So I had a brain tumor! A tumor. My father must have been syphilitic. And I knew nothing about it. That meant the end. I am finished and done for. I won't let them operate. Not on my head! They're not shoving my brain about. The devil knows what would become of me then. I want to stay as I am.

The clairvoyant had sat down. But he raised his uncanny white hand once again, soulful and threatening at the same time, threatening for me, although the others gazed at it as if he were God the father creating the world, like in Michelangelo's painting.

"Are you an animal lover?"

Of course, I thought to myself. I am an animal lover. Just

think how much I like sheep, I like seeing cows as well in the Alpine meadows. I can find white rabbits quite delightful. Dogs? I do not in fact like dogs. I find pigeons disgusting. I took a cat which adopted me straight to the Animal Protection League, so that I wouldn't have any bother. Perhaps I'm not such an animal lover after all. I sighed with relief. Maybe he was not quite right about the tumor either. It could just be an infection.

"I can see a room," he pronounced. "A writing desk. You are sitting in front of it. You are writing. You are wearing glasses. The left lens is stronger than the right."

I am a writer and I do wear glasses. Indeed the left lens was stronger. I shut my right eye, then my left. Obviously, everyone sees better with the left than with the right. I am no exception. That's because at school the light always comes from the left. But he says that in my case the left lens is stronger! I blushed. Right! I did see better with my right eye.

"I can see a second room. There is a picture. A portrait." He stood up. "Your father," he bellowed.

"Dazzling!" Minna said under her breath.

"You are closely attached to your father," he continued.

I suddenly calmed down completely. All my fear fell away at a stroke. I leaned back with a smile and nodded serenely.

"In your left jacket pocket is a diary," he said. I handed it to him. He ran his thin hands over it, stroking it. "On the fifteenth of January you have made an entry. It will help shape the rest of your life. Read it!"

I took the little book and opened the page.

"Read it out!"

"I can't do that," I said, biting my lip to stop myself from laughing.

"Thank you, that's enough," he said, gesturing me aside with his long white hand, making me feel I was being dismissed.

An opulent tea was served. The clairvoyant was exhausted and did full justice to the meal. I was amazed at how much he could put away. Another guest filled up his plate for him time after time. It was a guest from "Paradise." I deduced from the conversation that the guests belonged to a club which was called "Paradise." I found the name appropriate. They had all been driven from paradise: the lady pianist who never got a booking, Minna who had never married, Antonia who was far too tall, the deaf old lady who had too much zest for life for someone with her affliction. She did not hear anything the clairvoyant said but could "feel" his words.

"You could make millions with your divine gift," Antonia said emphatically.

"What do you mean, my dear?" he asked with an indulgent smile. I noticed how Antonia's expression became quite childish, how the whole burden of her height fell from her shoulders.

"If you teamed up with a financier, for example, and let him know in advance which stocks were going to rise in value, in return for a share of the profits, of course."

"Yes and you could become a philanthropist and serve humanity by founding hostels and homes for children and old people." This was Minna's dream.

At this the clairvoyant took out his watch and stood up quickly. Everyone was pleased to touch his hand.

"A charlatan!" I said as he shut the door behind him.

"How can you say that? Everything he said was right!" Minna expostulated.

"Remember that I was born after my father died."

"What do you mean?"

"I never knew my father and he never knew me."

"What's this?" shouted the deaf old lady.

"He hasn't got a father," the waiter shouted into her ear.

"Rubbish! That can't possibly be true."

"That was evidently a mistake," said the benefactor, turning to face me. "It shows that one must be skeptical. The mesmerist Klaas is incapable of making such mistakes. The powers he works with are honest. He doesn't make up any stories."

"But he hasn't made a mistake. It's all quite correct what he said. Of course you are closely attached to your father. Attachments to the dead are the closest of all. I don't understand how you dare criticize him in this way. You are insulting our club. You have no inkling of greatness when you speak like that," Minna said, offended.

"Here are the hands," the pianist had quickly fetched them, the mesmerist's waxen hands, which had at first given me such a fright. It was symbolic of everything which happened subsequently, a debilitating fright which then turned out to be fake.

"They are clever, sinewy hands," opined the art expert.

"And what can they do?"

"Touching them has a calming effect. I don't know if they have healing properties."

"One should be skeptical."

"Well, *you* won't heal us," Antonia called in my direction. "But would you be so kind as to show us the fateful note in your diary? It's not that I'm nosy, but it would be interesting to know what the master found out."

I took out my notebook, opened it to the fifteenth of January, and passed it to Antonia. She giggled into her handkerchief and handed it on to the pianist. Her nose grew even longer in bafflement and she passed it to the benefactor of the arts. He gave me a meaningful stare and gave the little book to the waiter. He let the circus rider see it first and she made a loud noise to indicate her astonishment. The deaf lady ripped it out of her hand, cast a glance inside, and hurled it at me in fury. The page was blank.

Notes

1. "Hellseher" by Veza Magd, first published 14 March 1937 in *Der Sonntag. Beilage des Wiener Tag*, reprinted in *Der Fund* (2001), pp.23-29.

Hush-Money. A Story from a High-Class Sanatorium[1]

The Baroness's hasty departure was on all the patients' lips at the Lilienhain Sanatorium. Just the day before she had assured the consultant that she wanted to stay, stay for a long time, indeed, and she asked him to make this clear to her husband. And then suddenly she had fled, leaving behind her apartment in the most dreadful state of untidiness. Upset bottles of perfume lay on the floor, items of underwear, clothes, scraps of paper or, so it appeared, scraps of a banknote, pieces of a mirror, gaming chips, bonnets, and crumpled ribbons.

The Lilienhain Sanatorium contains three categories of patients. Downstairs in the main room sit the psychiatric cases who have grey faces and stare into space. The seriously ill are to be found reclining in the lounge. But upstairs in their own rooms are those who are moderately ill, ladies each one of them. They keep to their beds and wear fragrant silk chemises, immaculately coiffed, freshly madeup, in a cloud of perfume - waiting for the consultant.

The consultant does his round three times a day. The seriously ill have need only of his skill. The psychiatric cases think of him more as a sort of guard to the madhouse. But those who are moderately ill demand everything.

The consultant sighs as he enters the room of the patient in number eight. Her bare arms lie wide apart on her pillows.

"How is your digestion?" asks the consultant and sits down in front of her. He usually begins with the appetite but this patient is too beside herself today. She does not answer and looks at him with damp eyes.

"What a rude question, Doctor!"

"Do you have a temperature?" He takes hold of her wrist.

"When you touch me!"

The consultant pulls out his watch and looks into space for a minute. Then he checks a graph.

"How is your appetite?"

"Abnormal," she says and devours him.

This makes the consultant smile his glassy smile and he takes her hand in both of his as he gets up, gets up in such a way as to suggest it costs a great act of will not to tear the sick woman away with him. And then he goes.

He relaxes when he gets to room number seven, for in room number seven lives the Baroness. The Baroness is very young and she too wants for nothing, but luckily a consultant is not her social equal. To his inquiry about appetite, she sticks out her tongue and when she hears the word "digestion" she turns away in disdain. But not today. Today the Baroness has undergone a transformation.

"No appetite?"

"Oh, yes!"

"Digestion?"

"Oh, please!"

"Temperature?"

"Oh, no!"

"You are doing somewhat better today," says the consultant, "but you mustn't walk about yet."

"Oh, but I am walking about. On the corridor. To room number one and back."

"Room number one," thinks the consultant. And he gets up contentedly.

"I must stay here for a long while yet, mustn't I?"

"At least another six weeks."

"Please do tell the Baron."

"Gladly. When is he coming?"

"He's not coming today. Today he's phoned. When he phones, he doesn't come." She winked mischievously. But as she had not done so at him, the consultant made a bow and smiled a contented smile, which this time he kept to himself.

The patient in number one, who was the object of the cunning glint in the Baroness's blue eyes, was an imposing gentleman with a tiny black moustache, who, for reasons which were known only to himself, always wore riding breeches. He was the object of more speculation among the patients in the Lilienhain Sanatorium than even the consultant. They said he was not seriously ill at all but had reasons for hiding himself away. Politics, whispered the psychiatric cases; on account of someone's husband, averred the moderately ill. Because of his splendid appearance they called him the Magnate. This Magnate had caught the Baroness's eye when she stepped out into the corridor in a state of delightful half-undress to look out for roomservice. The effect was mutual. And so it came about that at night when everyone was asleep the Baroness, wearing her little golden slippers, scurried as quietly as a mouse from room number seven to room number one, and nothing at all in her quick movements suggested she was moderately ill.

They so enjoyed each other's company that it was already bright daylight when an automobile pulled up outside the sanatorium. The Baroness jumped up to the window and stopped herself from letting out a cry. Then she skipped into her fur coat and flew back along the corridor, even faster than she had come. It goes without saying that she was lying in her bed, groggy with sleep, when her husband entered.

The Magnate in room number one had taken a bath, rung for the barber, put on his riding breeches, looked out of the window to check on the weather, seeing the Baron down below walking this way and that, and smiled. Then he put on three different ties, one after the other, throwing each one off in turn, and as he was tying the fourth, the chambermaid came into the room and set about airing his bed. He was following her movements in the mirror when suddenly his pulse missed a beat. For at that moment the chambermaid was extracting an item of lady's underwear from under the blankets, a poem of silk and lace. The Magnate bit his lip but retained his composure and said to himself, still looking in the mirror, that the sanatorium currently accommodated sixty patients, of whom forty-two were ladies, consequently the panties could not compromise any one of them individually. And as he was thinking this, the chambermaid was straightening out the underwear and she straightened out a seven-pointed crown, which was embroidered from behind in blue silk, and called out, in case there should still be any misunderstanding: "These panties belong to the Baroness!"

The Magnate still did not turn his gaze from the mirror but tried to read in the eyes of the chambermaid how big the danger was. He saw the girl blush at her own words, saw her innocent expression, and knew that he could sort everything out with a banknote. He clearly had no idea how discreet and well trained the chambermaids at the Lilienhain Sanatorium are. He thus took out a large banknote from his wallet, rolled it up, pressed it into the chambermaid's hand, pointed to the underwear and said without moving his lips:

"Return this discreetly to the lady."

"Really?" The chambermaid's astonishment knew no bounds, but she stuffed the panties into her skirt pocket, followed by the banknote, and hurried, still astounded, across the corridor to room number seven.

The Baroness had also been about her toilette and stood fully fragrant in front of the mirror with magnificent color in her cheeks. She pulled her coat over her shoulders in order to catch up with her husband, whom she had sent out to the park, and to charm him into making all manner of promises. Then the chambermaid came in and placed her panties before her. On top of the panties, she laid a one-hundred schilling note, said, a little disconcertedly, that the gentleman from number one had sent it, and departed hurriedly from the room, her eyes rooted to the floor.

This made the Baroness turn pale. She turned as pale as the paint on the wall. She felt her temples. She buried her face in her hands. She did not know what was coming over her. She knocked over the little dressing table and broke the mirror. She yanked open the chest and scattered the clothes about. She grabbed at a box and emptied its contents onto the floor. She hurled the panties into the corner along with the note for one-hundred schillings. She bent over, picked it up, and tore it with trembling fingers into a thousand pieces. Then she arranged her silver-fox fur, pulled on her hat, and tore down the stairs and into the park as if someone were chasing after her. Down in the avenue the Baron was waiting. With great delight he heard that she wanted to come with him right away. She did not even have the time to pack her bags. The maid could fetch everything later.

In the sanatorium everyone was talking about this bizarre departure. Only the chambermaid kept her mouth shut.

Notes

1. "Schweigegeld" by Veza Magd, first published 11 April 1937 in *Die Stunde*, reprinted in *Text und Kritik* (2002), pp.11-14.

Money - Money - Money. The Life of a Rich Man[1]

How frightened to death I was on the staircase! Could those four hours ever pass? Had it been possible to survive that week? Neighbours came up the stairs and looked at me curiously. They all knew what was going on. They must have spoken to me too, but I did not understand a thing of what was going on. I ran up and down the landing, ran up the stairs, down the stairs, and waited for him to come. My mother was going to bring him with her. He would be stocky with large dark eyes. He would look at my mother with these eyes and steal her heart from me and then look at me severely and scold me. I knew in advance that all this would happen, though I had not yet met him. Our lodger tried to fetch me back – yes, we had a lodger. We were poor. That is why this stepfather was coming. I turned my back on him. Never was a child as unhappy as I.

Then a man did come up the stairs, gaunt-looking, tall and thin, with an enormous nose and wearing a furcoat with a mink collar and a tall fez on his bald head. He was a Turk from Bosnia.[2] He carried a stick in his hand. His eyes were not large and dark, but rather small and colorless, as if he were blind. White stubble sprouted from his cheeks, and I knew that this was the stepfather. Suddenly all my feelings fell away, my disgust, my worry, my shame. I looked curiously at the gaunt old man following his stick up the stairs and behind him, young and lightfooted, my mother now appeared. She slid up to me, gave me a great hug, and whispered:

"You can call him papa or uncle."

"Uncle, of course," I said and my mother ran into the apartment.

When the stepfather saw me, he made his toothless mouth into a dark, gaping hole, and, pushing his tongue through his cheek, said "Aha!" Then he hit me on the leg with his stick, which was his way of showing affection.

The maid and the lodger did not laugh when they saw the peculiar old man, but stepped respectfully to one side, for he was the owner of forty-seven houses. My stepfather went into our front parlor, took off his fur, stepped out of his suit, got back into his fur, and spat on the carpet. Then he sank himself comfortably into an armchair, took a swig of liquor, which my mother had already put out for him, and demanded wine. To go with the wine he wanted meatpies, and while my mother, tired from the journey, went into the kitchen at ten o'clock at night and baked pies, he lit a cigar. As there was no fresh meat in the house, she filled them with minced sausage.

Meanwhile he drank alternately from two glasses, smoked, burrowed his tongue into his cheek as a sign of supreme contentedness, and looked around the room. The furniture was oldfashioned and illuminated by a kerosene lamp. As my stepfather owned forty-seven houses, my mother lit both the small standinglamps, as saving fuel really was not a problem any more. I meanwhile contemplated his long, bent nose and suddenly became curious about all the toys which the maid had told me he would bring. He seemed to guess what I was thinking. Smiling to himself, he reached into his pocket and took out a small piece of paper. He took his time unsticking a sweet from it and, with a regal gesture signifying his generosity, passed it to me between two long fingers.

By the time the pies came the room was filled with thick smoke. It was eleven o'clock and I was not yet in bed. Suddenly, this did not make me happy. Suddenly, I longed for a return of the old way of doing things which forced me into bed at eight.

But the old way of doing things was not going to come back. While we knew that the stepfather owned forty-seven houses, we did not know how he had acquired them. After a few weeks we moved into a large apartment with electric lighting and we had enough space, but we still all had to live in the same room, as he would not tolerate more than one lamp in the house. At lunchtime we would all sit at the table and my mother would pile up my plate. But if she placed that tiny piece of meat on top which a child of twelve needs, he would fix his colorless eyes on the tiny piece and say:

"She's getting meat!"

However kindly my mother would now look at me, I could not get the meat down and that is what he seems to have anticipated. He would skewer it onto his fork and place it with satisfaction onto his plate. Dessert had to be consumed secretly in the kitchen, as he did not tolerate dessert. He himself ate great amounts of meat, drank liquor and wine from the bottle, and defied the predictions of the doctors.

He would go out every afternoon. He slipped into his suit, wrapped himself in his fur, grabbed his walking stick, and set off. He gave the impression of poverty, as his fur was shabby and stained, the collar on his shirt was frayed, but he did not care. He would think to himself about his forty-seven houses with all the shops which also belonged to him and that he used up less than one-twentieth of the rents he received. He walked down our street until he came to a small bench which belonged to Trott the servant who was sitting on it. He whacked Trott the servant, on the back, which made him jump to his feet and, in a manner which was both subservient and solicitous at the same time, give up his seat to the old man, who had perhaps once seen better days. When the poor gentleman had rested, he gave the servant a condescending nod and left. He would then stop at the first fruit stall. Depending what the season was, he bought an eighth of a kilo of apples, cherries, or plums. The fat fruitwoman saw the starved skeleton with stubble on his old cheeks and gave him a quarter for the price of an eighth. Sometimes the cherries were so cheap that it was not even worth working out how much an eighth cost. Then she would give him the fruit and he smiled his secret smile and went off, despising the kindhearted fruitwoman because she gave away her wares for nothing. He went up to the bridge as far as the shoeshine man. He stretched out his enormous boots in front of him, as he loved making them shine more. He looked with contentment as the shoeshine man smeared a large dollop of paste on to the already clean boots, rubbed them first with one brush, then with another, first with a hard cloth, then with a soft one, until they shone like varnish. When the nabob then saw the successful result, he reached with two long fingers into the bag with the donated fruit and, with that regal gesture which signified generosity, he passed the shoeshine man the smallest apple as a reward. Satisfied, he would then begin his walk home.

At home he would take off his suit, put his fur back on, and sit himself down on his bed directly in front of the stove, wearing nothing - apart from his fez - but his shirt and underwear. He lit a cigarette, drank alternately from his two bottles, poked the fire, and rang for the maid. The maid was the daughter of a peasant from Styria.[3] Her face had a classical beauty. Every time she came into the room, my stepfather felt pleased that he could wear out so splendid a specimen, whose presence would have adorned a castle, by getting her to do his bidding.

"Coffee!" he commanded and the maid brought coffee.

"Water!" he called directly afterwards and she brought water. Five minutes later he called her again and asked for a glass on the lefthand side of the chest of drawers to be moved to the righthand side. He was forever dreaming up errands and tasks for her because it pained him so much to leave her unused while he was paying her wages. My mother would be sitting all this time at the window, mending his beggar's rags. In the end, she took pity on the maid and as a gesture of self-sacrifice pushed a little table in front of the stove so as to amuse him with a game of dominos; she was thirty years younger than he.

To begin with he was visited by my mother's numerous relatives. But quite soon they stopped coming. He only wanted to receive people who could talk on an equal basis about his forty-seven houses, and so soon there was only one person left, a compatriot of his, who appeared punctually once a week. Sweeping imperiously past my mother, she went up with a warm smile to her fellow countryman in his underclothes. They talked about their houses and, when it was the season, my stepfather inquired about the harvest.

"Why do you always ask about the harvest?" my mother wanted to know one day.

"Because if there is a good harvest, the peasants spend their money."

"But why do you need the peasants? The whole town buys from you?"

He made an artful expression.

"The peasants buy bad goods and pay high prices."

"Why don't you explain to them what they're doing?" I asked.

He gave me a stony stare.

"You will go a long way," he then said across the room to his visitor. My mother noticed his look which brimmed with unspeakable contempt, examined me anxiously, and sighed. The woman from Bosnia smiled maliciously. He was very satisfied with her visits. But then she lost her money. When she reappeared after a while looking rather crestfallen, he would not look up.

"You are a beggar now," he said, and with that she was dismissed. She crept past my mother and did not come again.

Once every year one of his children came to visit him. He adored them with that love which a ruler has for the heirs to his throne. He expected them to increase his fortune and they did increase it. His feelings for all of them were the same. After he had asked them how much money they had and how many children, he sent them away because he could not bear them sitting there in idleness when they could be doing business. For this reason, they did not feel those tender feelings for him which children otherwise feel for their parents. Rather they felt bewildered gratitude because he was doing all he could to bequeath them his riches.

Only one of his sons was not a chip off the old block. He was handsome and pale and looked like a shepherd. Rather than mistreating his tenants, he voluntarily reduced their rent, threw a silver coin to a beggar, spent all his income, and in the end got engaged to a poor girl. This made my stepfather sign a power of attorney and have this son taken to the mental asylum. When the colossal young man was locked up in a tiny room, where the table and chair were nailed down and the window had bars in front of it, he really began to go mad, ran into the wall with his head, broke his head open, and died.

My mother walked about with quivering lips und could not pass on the news to the old man. When she finally spoke, he assumed the expression of someone who was starving.

"Write to his bride this minute and demand back the presents," he said brusquely. Then he sat down in front of the stove and hid his face. However hard I studied his expression I could read nothing in it except satisfaction because the pest had been due a share of his fortune.

Our relatives, who had pushed my mother into marriage, were forever exhorting me to do what he said and be kind to him, as that would touch his heart. I took my savings out of my moneybox and looked for a present for him. It was a watch stand, a dainty object. At the press of a button a disk in the middle went round, a music box at the bottom played a waltz, and at the press of another button an electric bulb lit up. I used a special feast day as an excuse and, trembling with joy, handed the present to him.

He looked it over with delight. He turned it this way and that, pressed all the buttons, hung his watch on it, and burrowed his tongue through his cheek. But suddenly he seemed to remember something. His long face looked consumed with hunger, his dark lines appeared on his cheeks, and he pushed the small item far away from him.

"You must have lots of money if you can afford to buy

presents," he then said and shortly afterwards cut my mother's housekeeping allowance.

He frequently suffered strokes and doctors had to be called. They predicted he would die very soon. One by one they died themselves, but he recovered and, smiling his secret smile, carried on living on meat and alcohol.

Then the war years came.

"I gave you a thousand crowns. Do you know what a thousand crowns are?"

His long finger trembled in agitation, as he tapped his forehead and beseeched her. He looked like an imprisoned potentate whose captors were choking him with their demands.

"One thousand crowns are not worth a *single* crown," my mother said for the hundredth time. She tore up the money, in order to make him finally understand that it was worth nothing, nothing.

When he saw that she was tearing up money, he gave her a perturbed look. Then he buttoned his money better into his fur.

His large revenues were deposited with a banker whose bank grew and grew as a result. For the stepfather was speculating with the money and did not send the certificates to his children until they had been cashed. They were too busy with their properties to see the method in his mad behavior. We, on the other hand, were starving. On account of our poverty, a medical complaint of my mother's grew worse and she lay in bed seriously ill.

"Aha!" said the stepfather. "Aha! Illness is laziness! Get up! Get up! Do some work!" And he hit at her bed with his stick.

From this time onwards, my mother no longer stuck to her strict principles of doing her duty and started to go out after midday. As he had chased away his visitors, he now sat alone with nothing to do during the long afternoons, for he could not read. What's more from now on, we only let him have his own portion of meat. Thus, he now went hungry too.

When the maid's tall figure appeared in the doorway and the old man's colorless eyes glided agreeably over her shape, the desire to caress her rounded calves with something other than his stick took hold of him.

"The woman is hungry," the maid then said. Disgusted by such venality, he let her go.

For as long as the currency was unstable, we were hungry. But he was hungry as well. He became even more gaunt. His dry fingers moved quickly through the air. He was not dying of hunger. He was doing his figures. He was calculating how much his children earned from war contracts and he despised everything else.

It was not possible to get the better of him. We were just the unpaid helpers in his service. We starved and he revelled.

Each month his secretary brought him a statement on the stocks and shares that he had acquired over the years, and it gave him great pleasure to work out the income which accrued from them. The secretary, his own nephew, had earlier been the owner of almost all the houses which now belonged to the old man. But his motto was "honest lasts longest" and this turned out to be true. For after he had lost all his houses and his fortune, he was still left with his honesty. My stepfather, who had, one by one, stolen each of his houses in return for loans which the nephew could not pay back straightaway, hired him as secretary in compensation and did not care about his lack of industriousness because he did all his sums himself. When the secretary brought him the quarterly statement, presenting it tidily on top of a pile of bits of paper, it turned out that the old man had the figures in his head already, and it turned out too that the right sum was that calculated in the old man's head and the wrong one that which the secretary had worked out with so much effort.

One day the secretary arrived with a letter from a tenant and read it out:

Honored Landlord,
i, Kozil the shoemaker, am walking barefoot in my apartment,
that is because the ruffians have robbed my shop. When i go to the

authority and say but that is not right that i go to the war and they rob my shop they say they can do nothing and my wife should have lookd after it. How should she have lookd after it when she is lying in the hospital and, well then, the authority is not looking after it but the ill wife should look after it who has bad feet. When i come to the apartment everything is gone and i see the furniture at the neighbors and cannot do anything because they say i am a swabe.[4] But for the war i am not a swabe, now i have scratchd up a little together that i can work again but the rent is come now and now the misfortune is there. Honored Landlord, do not throw me into misfortune how should i pay, when i have scratchd together everything and i now start to work then i will pay for certain i will pay. For twentythree years i have payd on time how will i not pay this time. I just must start to work. I request very much Honored Landlord wait just a while until I have workd then i pay everything you will not throw me on to the street I have had the shop for twentythree years. I request very much and my wife sends her best wishes and kisses your hand.

Sarajevo 1919 in November

The secretary looked up with his kind expression and made an angelic appeal to my stepfather.

"But you must help him, Uncle. You are such a good person. Please help him." He laid his sweet, fat hand on the old man's bones. He was not being diplomatic when he called him kind. He himself was of such a pure temperament that for him the whole world was full of kind people. You just had to know how to treat them. I looked sympathetically at how he was *entreating.*

"Leave me in peace!" bellowed back my stepfather. "Look at yourself! Where you have got to! You are a beggar. Why are you bothering me with this? You can go to Hell."

But the secretary, who believed in the goodness of people, carried on entreating.

"Just this one quarter, this one quarter, Uncle. You wait and see. God will reward you for it."

"This one quarter," he mimicked back. "As if it were a question of one quarter! I get double the rent when the beggar moves out." His expression was burning with hunger as if he had been starving up to now because of the low rent.

"Write immediately that he has to move out."

"Of course, Uncle." His peaceful countenance remained undarkened. He folded up the letter and tucked it away. Then he bade a warm farewell and not a single thought on the problematic nature of human goodness crossed his mind. It was because thoughts never did cross his mind that he was so good.

My stepfather bored his tongue into his cheek in satisfaction, and just two weeks later received the news that the new tenant had moved in for double the rent. As a postscript was included the information that Kozil the shoemaker had hanged himself after his eviction.

The stepfather took the letter and threw it into the fire.

Meanwhile the general situation improved somewhat. The currency markets calmed down, and this affected us beneficially too. But it was now that our loyal maid, who had never let us down, went back home.

It was not easy to find a replacement at that time. The sons of the peasants lay dead on the battlefields which meant the daughters, whom they otherwise gladly send to the city, were in great demand.

Then the secretary brought a servant woman into the house, a compatriot of my stepfather. We got a fright when we went into the hall to greet her. Before us stood a mask. She gave off a dull, lifeless glow from beneath pitch-black hair, two small pitch-black eyes moved as if they really were looking out from behind a disguise. Her features were regular and broad. Everything about her was broad. Her face had acquired breadth, her back was broad, her hips were so broad that it looked as if she could prop her arms on them. She was called Draga. When Draga spoke, she gave a look of such ostentatious innocence that one wondered why she was so importunate at showing how innocent she was. As a rule, however, her eyes were hidden behind thick bulges of flesh. She worked like a machine. She learned our habits by listening and did everything herself as if she had taken a vow to bear all our burdens on her own shoulders.

She showed particular zeal with my stepfather. Before he had emptied one bottle of cognac, she fetched a new one. She ordered him the most powerful wine from the secretary. She brought him the strongest cigars, and if my stepfather pinched the tiniest piece of meat from her plate, she gave him her entire portion. And he, who had not liked her at first, the exchange of a flourishing beauty for a faded one having upset him, grew so used to her that soon he could not do without her.

We soon could not do without her either. For even though we suspected she was in league with the old man, we were fascinated by her. She never spoke about herself. Nothing surprised her. My mother's strange marriage seemed natural to her. We liked her, but she did not like us. She put on her good, demure expression if she looked us in the eye, but in other respects she was furtive. And she was particularly furtive, so it seemed to me, in the way she took no notice of my stepfather.

She never complained. But she was consumed by a secret passion and a secret plan. Yes, we feared her.

Only the stepfather was at ease with her. He smiled to himself when she brought him pies, strong coffee, spicy meals, and heavy wine. And if my mother reprimanded her, for the hot seasonings were poison for the elderly man, she lowered her eyes shiftily.

My mother diluted the wine. Draga changed over the bottles. My mother added mild seasonings to the hot ones. Draga threw them away and bought new ones. My mother hid the cigars. Draga found them and brought them triumphantly to the old man. My mother scolded her. Draga remained obstinate. She kept a close eye on us. She suspected us for no reason. Even if she did ingratiate herself with him, we knew precisely how little reward it would bring her.

It was strange but she seemed to value this job, where she was badly paid, granted no privileges, where an elderly man reduced her food, her wages, her free time, her meager pleasures. The more she let him take from her, the more he took. And the more he exploited her, the more she served him. We never saw her laugh, though.

This comfortable life which a servant provided him suited him so well that he now loved his loneliness fanatically. It did not cost him anything. He no longer went out and even saved on fruit. He no longer toyed with my mother and did not waste a penny on her. He calculated what he was saving on fools' pleasures. And he turned out the lights and saved on light.

Whenever we gently encouraged him to take a walk, Draga would immediately be standing behind us. Now life would come into her disguise. She spoke animatedly and for so long that she won the argument and he stayed at home. She gave him the feeling that he was appreciated. And he stayed at home and his loneliness made him so sensitive that he jumped in fright whenever we came into the room. And we felt that we were a nuisance to him and avoided his room.

One day, though, my mother did ask me to look in. She watched me anxiously as I did so.

The old man was sitting bent over the fire. Lines were forming on his left temple, which became pressed into the shape of a triangle, betraying his monstrous effort. He was staring into the fire which must have been burning his eyes.

"Gold, gold," he said.

"The sacks are full of gold!" He was in a state of awestruck excitement.

"Yes, the fire looks like gold."

I thought at first of shapes which he could see in the fire, as we see shapes on the moon, and wondered to myself at this uncharacteristic deviation from reality.

"The whole day long they are carrying in gold." He was

trembling. "There! There they are again!"

"Uncle, we can't get inside the stove. It's too small."

"That's what I've been wondering about for weeks." He wrinkled up his face into its new tormented pattern. "They often bring in diamonds, sacks full of diamonds. There! Do you see them? Officers. The uniforms are gold. Gold!"

I tried to look him in the face. He looked at me. His eyes were gentle.

"Do they go on for the whole day?"

"The whole day," he said awestruck.

"What if I were to close the door?" and I closed the door.

"No, don't do that, don't. I have to see them." He opened the door again carefully.

As these apparitions of people with gold and jewelery gave him more pleasure than pain, I reassured my mother. I thought to myself that nature was compensating him for his self-denial.

But a couple of weeks later we heard him banging about. When I went in, he was poking furiously around in the coals with the poker.

"Get out, get out!" he screamed.

Then he let out a sigh and to my very great astonishment threw a silver coin into the flames.

"Uncle, why are you throwing money into the fire?"

"You have to."

"What do you have to do?"

"You have to give it to them."

"Who do you have to give it to?"

He did not say anything. His forehead was damp.

"Don't you want to close the door a little bit, Uncle?"

"Yes, let's close the door." He sighed with relief. I spoke to him to distract his attention.

"There. There you have him!" He pointed with his stick into the corner. It was uncanny to watch him hitting with his stick into the empty corner.

"Nobody is there, Uncle, he's gone, I've chased him away."

He did not look at me until I had set foot into the empty corner. Then he burst out laughing.

"Do you think I'm a child? There he is! There he is! There he is!"

"I can see him too. There he is!" Behind us stood Draga.

"Draga," I shrieked. "What are you saying? You'll make him more confused. Go away."

She turned on her heels and went.

"What does he want then, when he stands there, Uncle?"

He calmed down. I tiptoed out. I had to see Draga. I had to ask her.

But when I stood before her, I could not open my mouth. Her expression had turned to stone. It was cold, lifeless, like a disguise. I went to my stepfather. Opening the door quietly, I saw how he was taking a packet out of his toppocket. He unwrapped lots of little brown bundles. Twenty-schilling notes were inside. Before I could come up to him, my step-father took the banknotes and threw them as quick as lightning into the fire. I hurled myself at the fire, but he stopped me. He held me back with the poker. He had suddenly acquired the strength of a giant. I had to look on helplessly as the valuable notes glowed, burst into flames. Now there were just a few left. It shot through my head that perhaps some would be left at the end, but my stepfather poked the valuable scraps about in the fire until they disintegrated. I thought about the many things we did without. I would have burned my fingers to save something. He was visibly satisfied.

Over the next little while, one little packet after another disappeared without our being able to prevent it, as he carried his money about with him day and night. But the old man himself was wasting away too. His body shook with indeterminate fear. My mother saw the heart-rending transformation, forgot the years of pain, the humiliations, the worry, her grievances, and did not leave his side, but she could not scare off the apparitions. The fear was choking him.

One night he began to talk about the dead. He counted up all the dead in his life, his dead parents, his dead siblings, his dead son, his dead friends. He counted them up and told their stories. I knew that he was going to die.

"He's going to die," I said to the doctor. "We have to get in touch with his children."

"He's not going to die," said the doctor.

"How can he possibly die!" Draga was standing behind us.

"He's going to die," I said, "because he's talking about the dead. He doesn't normally talk about the dead." I wrote to his children.

Draga wrote to his children too. She told them that there was not any danger, especially as he was getting a course of injections. The children did not come, and my stepfather carried on telling stories. He counted up his numerous children, and when he mentioned his youngest son, he hesitated.

"He's coming," he said, "he's coming to see me."

"Of course he'll come," I reassured him and I wrote a second letter.

Draga wrote another letter too and noone came.

One night the old man got up and staggered to the door. My mother and I held him back. Draga supported him too, but then I looked into Draga's face.

"Get out, Draga," I said.

My stepfather fell to the floor. The same night I sent a telegram to his youngest son and he came. He was not sentimental and came banging genially into the room. But when he saw the emaciated face, his good mood was over. He sat down at the bedside and held the dying man's hand.

He had suddenly become his old self again. He thought of his large fortune which was safe in the hands of his children. He thought contentedly that my mother was not getting anything and when he looked up, his eyes were pained to see the bright furniture. His expression become hungry.

"Take the furniture away from her," he said to his son.

"I will take everything away from her," he promised and asked my mother's forgiveness with his eyes.

The same day he fell into a coma. His groaning caused the inhabitants of the big house to come running all at once. They were all made to think of death. Draga was the exception. Her expression was calmness itself.

When his tough old heart finally stopped beating, Draga looked with curiosity at his tormented body.

A great number of people came to pay my stepfather their last respects at the funeral. They were friends of his sons, the wealthy heirs.

As the coffin was lowered, they took the shovel in turn and Draga took it too. She cast the earth into the grave as if she were sprinkling salt into the soup.

"Aren't you at all sorry, Draga, because of the gentleman?"

"It happens to all of us," she said coldly.

At this, I could no longer restrain myself. At home, while the guests were filling up the house, I sent Draga on an errand. Then I made my way to her room and searched through her chest. The drawers bent under the weight of clean linen, which maids cannot usually afford. I opened a locked compartment with a skeleton key. I found numerous, very tender letters in imperfect German. I recognized this German. The letters were from Draga's husband. This is how they were signed: "I, your husband, the shoe maker Kozil."

Next to the compartment was a cigar box. It was sealed on all sides and I did not dare to tear it open. I quickly fetched a knife from the kitchen and cut out the bottom. I pulled out what turned out to be an old noose. Nothing else. But there, there on the noose I saw the glitter of gold. A ring. A wedding ring, tied on to the long noose. And now I suspected something.

I called the secretary. He was with the mourners and was talking to my mother to help her drive the dark thoughts from her mind after the funeral. He was stroking her hand in kindness. I pulled him away and led him to Draga's room. I decided to set a trap for him.

"Do you know this picture?" I said and took a yellowing photograph out of the letter compartment.

"Isn't that ... yes, that is Kozil the shoemaker. But what are you doing, my dear? You mustn't do that."

"How long has he been dead, Kozil the shoemaker?"

"Not long." He was becoming more and more embarrassed.

"You mustn't do that, my dear. Come away from here."

"Why did he hang himself?"

"Did she tell you about it?" he asked anxiously.

I nodded. "She told me about it."

He looked around in fear.

"She isn't in the house."

"Come away from here and put all this back where it belongs, my dear."

"She's in despair about it. But why did he hang himself?"

"Well, because your uncle evicted him, of course. We were supposed to throw him on to the street. He couldn't pay the rent."

I gasped. "And so you brought Draga to us!"

"I wanted to help her, my dear."

"And so you brought her to us! Do you know what she has done? She has poisoned my stepfather - intentionally. She fed him with all the poisons which were bound to destroy him - all the poisons which he was strictly forbidden. She ensured him a terrible end! A horrifying death!"

"But what are you talking about, my dear? She's such a good person," he said, suspecting nothing.

He helped me tidy up Draga's chest. We agreed to keep the matter secret.

I now regarded Draga with great respect. She just waited for an appropriate length of time to pass and then went back to her hometown.

Notes

1. "Geld - Geld - Geld. Das Leben eines reichen Mannes" by Veza Magd, first published 1 May 1937 in *Die Stunde*, reprinted in *Text und Kritik* (2002), pp.15-27. The story shows remarkable similarities to the chapter "Patriarchs" in *The Torch in the Ear*, though Elias appears to have been unaware of the story when he was writing his autobiography. The behavior of Veza's own stepfather, Menachem Alkaley, who died in 1929, influenced both his depiction of the domestic murderer, Benedikt Pfaff, in *Auto-da-Fé* and Veza's account of Herr Iger in *The Ogre*. Alkaley cut his stepdaughter out of his will, in revenge, Elias believes, for her "taming" of him, which meant she and her new husband had to move out of the Ferdinandstraße after her mother's death in October 1934.

2. Spanish-speaking (Sephardic) Jews were called Turks, as after the Catholic Reconquest of Spain in 1492 they had been welcomed into the Ottoman Empire, to which the capital of Bosnia-Herzegovina, Sarajevo, belonged until the Congress of Berlin in 1878, which placed the province under Austro-Hungarian administration. It remained under Turkish "suzerainty" until 1908 when it was annexed by Austria-Hungary.

3. A rural province of Austria. Viennese maids tended not to come from the city itself but from the provinces or farther flung corners of the former Habsburg Empire. The second maid, who shares the first name Draga (meaning *dear* in Hungarian) with Mrs. Iger in *The Ogre*, comes from Sarajevo, like Canetti's own maternal relatives. As the stepfather's nemesis she is one of Canetti's two alter egos in the story, the other being the more timid narrator, who is shocked by Draga's actions before she realizes she approves of them.

4. From the province of Swabia in southwest Germany. The shoemaker Kozil is being accused by Bosnian Serbs of being descended from German settlers, thus loyal to Austria-Hungary which had declared war on Serbia on 28 July 1914 after the assassination on 30 June by a Serbian nationalist of the heir to the throne, Archduke Franz Ferdinand, in Sarajevo. The descendants, now a tiny handful in number, of a colony of ethnic Germans dating to the mid-thirteenth century in the Banat

region of Rumania are still known as the "Banat Swabians." In the eighteenth century, three so-called "Swabian Tracks" of 1722-26, 1763-73, and 1782-87 brought tens of thousands of German settlers to what are today Croatia, Serbia, and Bosnia-Herzegovina, as well as to Hungary and Rumania. Swabian thus became a term denoting all ethnic Germans. Kozil's next comment "but for the war I was not a swabe" suggests that he fought with Serbia against the German-speaking (and thus "Swabian") Austrians.